There were structures of stone and glass and gleaming metal. Jagged-edged turrets erupted from asymmetrical buildings. Strange lights blazed in the windows of huge stone monoliths. Low domes glimmered with pearl-like translucency. In the center of everything, a spiked tower of gleaming copper reached up to touch the sky. And everywhere, hanging lightly between the oppressive shapes and buildings, were frothy strands of gossamer walkways.

"It's a city," said Hunter, his voice awed and hushed. Then the first flush of excitement died down, and he found that his skin was crawling, and he had to keep fighting down an urge to look away. The shapes of the structures were ugly, twisted . . . *wrong*, somehow . . .

✛

Praise for Simon R. Green's
HAWK & FISHER series, the rousing
adventures of a swordsman
and a sorceress . . .

"GOOD FUN!"
—*Isaac Asimov's Science Fiction Magazine*

"INTRIGUE AND MAGIC . . . AN INTERESTING AND WELL-CONCEIVED BLEND."
—*Science Fiction Chronicle*

Ace Books by Simon R. Green

The Hawk & Fisher Series

HELLWORLD

SIMON R. GREEN

ACE BOOKS, NEW YORK

If you purchased this book without a cover, you should be aware that this book is stolen property. It was reported as "unsold and destroyed" to the publisher, and neither the author nor the publisher has received any payment for this "stripped book."

This book is an Ace original edition,
and has never been previously published.

HELLWORLD

An Ace Book / published by arrangement with the author

PRINTING HISTORY
Ace edition / September 1993

All rights reserved.
Copyright © 1993 by Simon R. Green.
Cover art by Sanjulian.
This book may not be reproduced in whole or in part,
by mimeograph or any other means, without permission.
For information address: The Berkley Publishing Group,
200 Madison Avenue, New York, NY 10016.

ISBN: 0-441-32599-8

ACE®
Ace Books are published by The Berkley Publishing Group,
200 Madison Avenue, New York, NY 10016.
ACE and the "A" design
are trademarks belonging to Charter Communications, Inc.

PRINTED IN THE UNITED STATES OF AMERICA

10 9 8 7 6 5 4 3 2 1

The sleep of reason brings forth monsters.

✟

CHAPTER ONE

Broken Men

THE starship *Devastation* dropped out of hyperspace and moved into orbit around Wolf IV. The planet's surface was hidden from view by the swirling atmosphere. It looked much like any other planet; a drop of spit against the darkness. The ship's sensor spikes shimmered briefly as it scanned Wolf IV, and then the cargo-bay doors swung open. A slender Navy pinnace emerged, sleek and silver, and drifted away from the huge bulk of the starship. The pinnace fell into its own orbit, and the *Devastation* disappeared back into hyperspace. The pinnace slowly circled the storm-shrouded planet, a gleaming silver needle against the star-speckled night.

Captain Hunter gnawed at the insides of his cheeks as he ran his hands over the control panels. It looked like he was going to have to pilot the ship down after all. This far out, the onboard computers were all but useless. They didn't have enough information to work with. Hunter shrugged. What the hell; it had been a long time since he'd had to fly a ship by the seat of his pants, but some things you never forget. Particularly if your life depends on them.

For a moment, the old overpowering uncertainty was suddenly back with him; the familiar panic of not being able to choose between alternatives for fear of doing the wrong thing. His breathing and heartbeat speeded up, and then slowed again as he fought grimly for control. He'd done this before, he could do it again. He ran through the standard instrument checks, losing himself in routine. The control panels blazed with steady, comforting lights. He checked that the pinnace's orbit was still stable, and

1

then released the sensor drones. Hunter watched them fall towards the planet on his viewscreen. The sensor probes had better tell him what he needed to know the first time; the odds were he wouldn't get a chance to launch a second series. It wouldn't be long now before the pinnace's orbit began to decay, and then he'd have to power up the engines, ready or not. The ship's batteries only had so much power, and he was going to need most of it for the landing.

Captain Scott Hunter was an average-looking man in his late twenties. Average height, average build, perhaps a little leaner than most. Dark hair, and darker eyes. There were never more than 500 Captains of the Imperial Fleet; the best of the best. At least, that was the official version. In reality, the only way to become a Captain was through money, power, or family influence. Hunter was a Captain because his father had been one, and his father before him. Scott Hunter, however, was one of the few who'd earned his position by virtue of training and ability. Which made it even harder to understand why he'd panicked during a rebel encounter above one of the Rim worlds, and lost his ship and half his crew as a result.

If he had died in the encounter, no one would have censured his behaviour. He would have been posthumously promoted to Admiral, and his Clan would have honoured his memory. But he'd survived, and so had enough of his officers to point the finger of blame. He could have resigned his commission, but he'd had enough pride left that he couldn't do that and shame his family. High Command asked him to explain his conduct, but he couldn't do that either. He didn't understand it himself. In the end, he was told he could either volunteer for the Hell Squads, or be cashiered. He chose the Hell Squads.

It wasn't much of a choice.

The pinnace's drones hurtled down through the turbulent atmosphere, absorbing what punishment they could and ignoring the rest. The probes weren't expected to last long anyway. Their sensor spikes glowed crimson from the increasing heat, but did not wilt. Information flowed back to the pinnace's computers in a steady stream as the drones fell endlessly through the thickening atmosphere.

Hunter tried to ease himself into a slightly more comfortable position in his crash webbing. He'd never cared much for webbing. There was no doubt it offered extra protection during rough landings, but he could never get his balance right. He'd never been any good in a hammock, either. He scowled unhappily, and clung surreptitiously to the control panels with one hand, while the other channelled incoming data through the navigational computers. He glanced across at his co-pilot.

"Get ready for data flow. I'm patching in our comm implants."

"Understood, Captain. Ready when you are." The Investigator's voice was calm and even, but then it always was.

Investigator Krystel was a striking-looking woman. She was barely into her mid-twenties, but her eyes were much older. She was tall and lithely muscular, and her sleek dark hair was pulled back into a tight bun, accentuating her high-boned face without softening the harsh lines. Her occasional lovers thought her handsome rather than pretty. Krystel rarely thought about it. She was an Investigator, trained by the Empire since childhood to be loyal, efficient, and deadly. Her job was to study newly discovered alien species and determine how much of a threat they might pose to the Empire. Depending on her findings, the aliens would then either be enslaved or exterminated. There was never any third option. Investigators were cold, calculating killing machines. Unofficially, they were often used as assassins in inter-Clan feuds.

Hunter wasn't sure how he felt about Krystel. He'd never worked with an Investigator before. Her training and experience would make her invaluable when it came to keeping the Squad alive on the new planet, but he didn't know if he could trust her. There were those who claimed Investigators were as inhuman as the aliens they studied. Because of who and what they were, Investigators were allowed a hell of a lot of leeway in the Empire. Hunter didn't even want to think what Krystel must have done to merit being banished to the Hell Squads. He didn't think

he'd ask. Investigators weren't known for their openness.
There was a soundless chime in his head, and he closed
his eyes and leaned back in his webbing as the ship's
computers patched him in with the probes.

Bright flashes of light and color filled his eyes, and wind
and static roared in his ears. The comm implant tied directly
into his optic and auditory nerves so that he could see and
hear firsthand what the probes were picking up, but it took
time before he and the computers could sort out the useful
information from the garbage. Hunter's mind meshed with
the computers, and his thoughts flowed among the surging
information at inhuman speed, sifting and examining the
rush of raw data. Brief glimpses of cloud and sky were
interspersed with drop velocities and wind speeds. Weather
projections were crowded out by flashes of sea and land
impossibly far below. Shifting landing probabilities flared
and guttered like candles in a wind. Hunter concentrated,
shutting out everything but the bare essentials. The computers were recording everything, and he could replay the
rest later.

He sensed the Investigator beside him in the computer
net; a cold, sharp image that reminded him of a sword's
cutting edge. He wondered fleetingly what he looked like
to her, and then concentrated on the probes as they fell
past the cloud layers and started showing him detailed
views of the land mass below. At first, they formed a con-
fusing mosaic of overlapping images, but Hunter quickly
relearned the knack of concentrating on each image for the
split second it took to register, and then passing on to the
next.

Wolf IV had one huge continent surrounded by storm-
tossed oceans. The land was composed of endless shades of
green and brown and grey, stained here and there with ugly
patches of yellow. There were towering mountain ranges
and vast lakes. Volcanic activity filled the air with ash,
and molten lava burned crimson and scarlet against the
broken earth, like so many livid wounds in the planet's
surface. There were large areas of woodland and jungle,
though the colors were all wrong, and huge stretches of

open grassland. Hunter focused in on one of the larger open areas. It looked as good a place as any to land, and better than most.

"Not a very hospitable world, Captain." The Investigator's voice was sharp and clear in his ear, rising easily over the probes' input.

"I've seen worse," said Hunter. "Not often, I'll admit, but then it's not as if we have a choice in the matter. Hang on to your webbing, Investigator. I'm taking us down. Probe seventeen, sector four. See it?"

"Looks good to me, Captain."

Hunter shut down his comm implant, and surfaced abruptly from the computer net. The dully lit control deck replaced the probes' visions as his eyesight returned to normal. He rubbed tiredly at his eyes. The landing site had looked good. It wouldn't have hurt his confidence any if Krystel had sounded a little more enthusiastic, but perhaps that was expecting too much from an Investigator. He squeezed his eyes shut for a moment. Direct input always gave him a headache. It was purely psychosomatic, but the pain felt real enough. He opened his eyes and stretched uncomfortably, careful of his balance in the webbing. After the sweeping views the probes had shown him, the control deck seemed more cramped and confined than ever.

Hunter and the Investigator lay in their crash webbing in the middle of a solid steel coffin. Dark, featureless walls surrounded them on all sides, with barely enough room for them both to stand upright. Presumably the designer's idea was that if the pinnace crashed on landing, all you had to do was bury it where it fell. Hunter pushed the thought firmly to one side and ran his hands over the control panels again. The main engines sent a low, throbbing note through the superstructure, and the pinnace began its long fall towards the planet.

The ship shook and shuddered violently as it entered the turbulent atmosphere, held on course only by the unrelenting thrust of the engines. Hunter swung from side to side in his webbing, but his hands were sure and steady on the controls. There was no trace now of the treacherous panic that at times overwhelmed him, and he ran confidently through the routines as old skills and memories came back to him. He tapped into the navigational computers through his comm implant, and the ship came alive around him. The pinnace's sensors murmured at the back of his mind, feeding him a steady flow of information, enabling him to anticipate and outmanoeuvre the worst batterings of the storm winds. Down below, the probes were dying one by one, burning up in the atmosphere or shattered by the storms. Hunter watched sympathetically as, one after another, their lights went out on the control panels. They'd been useful, but he didn't need them anymore. They'd served their purpose.

Outside the pinnace, the winds shrieked and howled. Warning lights flared on the control panels. The pinnace had lost some of its sensor spines, and the outer hull was breached somewhere back of the stem. Hunter keyed in the auxiliary systems for more power to the engines, and hoped they'd last long enough to get the ship down. It was going to be a near thing. He patched briefly into the probes again, but most of them were gone now. The few remaining drones hurtled towards the ground like shining meteors. Hunter braced himself instinctively as the ground rushed up towards him, and winced as one by one their transmissions suddenly shut down. He dropped out of direct input and studied the control panels. He'd have to rely on what was left of the pinnace's sensors to get him down now. Assuming they lasted long enough. He patched into them again via the navigational computers, and quickly located the wide-open space he'd chosen earlier. The details were blurred now by the pinnace's speed, but it didn't look anywhere near as inviting as it had from orbit. Desolate bloody area, in fact. Still, it would have to do. There wasn't time to choose another one. The ship lurched wildly as the winds hit it from a new angle, and Hunter fought to keep the descent steady. There was a shriek of tortured metal as another of the pinnace's sensor spines was ripped away.

"Attention in the rear! Brace yourselves!" Hunter yelled through his comm implant. "We're going in!"

He split his attention between the sensors and the controls, and fought to keep his feel of the ship alive. It wasn't enough to just work the controls; he needed to feel the ship as a part of himself and react accordingly, his instincts making decisions faster than his mind ever could. And then the ground came leaping up to meet him, and the pinnace hit hard, shaking and jarring the cabin. The landing gear howled as it strove to absorb the impact, and then everything was suddenly still and quiet. Hunter and the Investigator hung limply in their crash webbing. The control deck lights faded and then brightened again. Hunter waited for his heart and breathing to slow down a little, then reached out a shaking hand and hit the disconnects, powering down the engines. Might as well hang on to whatever power they had left. He sat up slowly and looked around him. The ship seemed to have come through intact, and the Investigator looked as calm and unshakable as ever.

"All right," Hunter said hoarsely. "Systems checks and damage reports. Give me the bad news, Investigator."

"Outer hull breached in three, four places," said Krystel, studying her panels. "Inner skin still secure, air pressure steady. Landing gear . . . battered but intact. The sensors are out. We lost too many spines on the way down. Apart from that, systems are running at eighty percent efficiency."

"One of my better landings," said Hunter. "Switch to the backup sensors. See what they have to tell us."

Krystel nodded, and her hands moved surely over the panels before her. Hunter patched into the comm net again. At first, there was only static, and then the outside scene filled his eyes. A patchy fog seethed around the pinnace, milky and luminous in the ship's outer lights. Beyond the light there was only darkness, an endless, unrelieved gloom without moon or stars. For as far as the sensors could show, the pinnace stood alone on an empty plain. Hunter dropped out of the comm net and sat thoughtfully in silence for a moment. It should be light soon. Perhaps their new home would look more attractive in the daylight. It could have looked a lot worse. Somehow, the thought didn't cheer him as much as he'd hoped. He looked across at Krystel. The Investigator was rerunning the records from the probes on the main viewscreen, and making extensive use of the fast-forward and the freeze frame. Hunter decided to leave her to it. He leaned back in his webbing and activated his comm implant.

"This is the Captain. We're down, and more or less intact. Everyone all right in the rear?"

"We're all fine, Captain. Just fine." The warm and reassuring voice belonged to Dr. Graham Williams. Hunter had met him briefly before the drop. Dr. Williams had an impressive record, a confident manner, and a firm handshake. Hunter didn't trust him. The man smiled too much. "The trip down was a trifle bumpy, but nothing the crash webbing couldn't handle. What does our new home look like, Captain?"

"Bleak," said Hunter. "Esper DeChance, run a standard scan of the area. If there's any living thing within a half-mile radius, I want to know about it right now."

There was a brief pause, and then the telepath's voice murmured calmly in his ear. "There's nothing out there, Captain. Not even any plant life. From the feel of it, you've dropped us right in the middle of nowhere."

"I've just had a great idea, Captain." That was one of the marines, Russel Corbie. His voice was sharp and hurried. "Let's turn this crate around and tell the Empire the whole damned planet was closed for renovations."

"Sorry, Corbie," said Hunter, smiling in spite of himself. "We pretty much drained the ship's batteries just getting down here. There's no way she'll ever be lifting into orbit again."

"So we're stuck here," said Corbie. "Great. Just bloody marvellous. I should have deserted when I had the chance."

"You did," said Hunter. "That's how you ended up in the Hell Squads."

"Besides," said Lindholm, the other marine, "even if we got upstairs again, what good would it do us? You don't suppose the *Devastation* is still there waiting for us, do you? She's long gone, Russ. We're on our own now. Just like they said."

The marine's words seemed to echo ominously. No one else said anything. The quiet seemed strange, almost eerie, after the chaos of the trip down. Now there was only the slow ticking of the cooling metal hull, and the occasional quiet murmur from the computers as the Investigator studied the main viewscreen. Hunter stretched slowly in his webbing, scowling unhappily as he tried to get a grip on what he should do first. There were any number of things he should be doing, but now that the moment had come he found he was strangely reluctant to act, as though by committing himself to any one action, the marooning of the pinnace would suddenly become fixed and real.

Hunter had had a lot of time to get used to the idea of being abandoned on Wolf IV, but somehow it had never seemed real before. Even on the morning before the drop, he'd still been half expecting a reprieve, or a standby, or something to happen that would mean he didn't have to go. But there was no reprieve, and deep down he'd known there wouldn't be. His Clan had turned its back on him. As far as they were concerned, he was already dead. Hunter bit his lower lip as the implications came home to him with new force.

There wasn't going to be any backup. The only high tech the Squad had was what they'd brought with them, and that would last only as long as the energy crystals that powered it. If anything went wrong, there was no one they could call on for help. They were alone on Wolf IV. The first colonists wouldn't be on their way for months, even assuming Wolf IV checked out as habitable. Long before then, the Hell Squad would either become completely self-sufficient, or they would all die.

On the other hand, there was no one here to interfere, either. For the first time in his career, Hunter had a completely free hand. On Wolf IV, there were no stupid rules and regulations to work around, no more having to bow and scrape to fools in high office. Hunter felt a little of the tension go out of him. He could cope. He always had, in the past. And the blind, unreasoning panic that had robbed him of his career and his future was just another obstacle he'd learn to overcome in the days ahead. He believed that, with all his heart. He had to. The alternative was unthinkable. He cut that line of thought short. He'd known what he was getting into when he volunteered.

The Hell Squads were one-way planet scouts. They landed on newly discovered worlds, searched out the good and bad points, and decided whether or not the place was colonizable. And learned how to stay alive while they were doing it. The Squads had a high mortality rate, which was why they were made up of people who wouldn't be missed. The expendable. The losers. The failures, the rebels, the outcasts, and the damned. Broken men and forsaken heroes. The people who never fitted in. Whatever happened on the world they went to, there was no way back. The new world was their home, and would be for the rest of their lives.

Hunter turned to Krystel, who was scowling at one of her monitor screens. "Tell me the bad news, Investigator."

"A lot of the details are still unclear, Captain, but I think I've got the general picture. There's been a lot of volcanic activity around here in the recent past, and it's still going on in some places. The air is full of floating ash, but it's breathable. It's too early yet to start worrying about long-term effects on the lungs, but it might be advisable to rig up some kind of masks or filters before entering the worst areas. Apart from that, all in all the signs look good. Air, gravity, and temperature are all within acceptable limits, as promised. Not a particularly pleasant world, but habitable."

"What can you tell me about the immediate vicinity?" said Hunter, frowning. "Anything to worry about there?"

"Hard to say, Captain. The sun won't be up for another hour or so, and there's some heavy mists. This planet has three moons, but none of them are big enough to shed much light. We'll have to wait till morning, and then go outside and look for ourselves."

"That isn't proper procedure," said the marine Corbie quickly, his voice breaking in through the comm net. "First man out is a volunteer job; always has been. And I want to make it very clear that I am not volunteering. First rule of life in the Service: never volunteer for anything. Right, Sven?"

"Right," said Lindholm.

"Keep the noise down," said Hunter. "I'm going to be the first man out."

He shook his head ruefully as the others fell silent. He should have made sure he was out of the comm net before discussing the situation with the Investigator. Not that Corbie's attitude had been much of a surprise. He'd better keep an eye on that one. He was going to be trouble. Hunter sighed, and clambered awkwardly out of his webbing. Might as well take a look now. He'd feel better once he was actually doing something. There was just room enough to stand up straight without banging his head on the overhead, and a few steps brought him to the arms locker. Krystel got out of her webbing to help him, and the two of them manoeuvred carefully in the confined space of the control deck.

First man out meant a full field kit. The steelmesh tunic went on first. Heavy enough to stop or turn a blade, but still light enough to let him move quickly and easily when he had to. Next came the gun and holster. Hunter felt a little easier with the disrupter on his right hip. The familiar weight was a comfort. The sword and its scabbard went on his left hip. The disrupter was a far more powerful weapon, but the sword was more reliable. The gun's energy crystal took two minutes to recharge between each shot. A sword never needs recharging. Next came a leather bandolier that crossed his chest, carrying half a dozen concussion grenades. Nasty things, particularly in a confined space. Hunter had always found them very useful. And finally, he snapped a force shield bracelet round his left wrist. He was now ready to face whatever the planet had to offer. In theory, anyway.

He rocked back and forth on his heels, getting used to the change in his weight. It had been a long time since he'd had to wear full field kit. Normally a Captain stayed safely in orbit, while his shock troops got on with the rough stuff down below. *Rank hath its privileges.* Hunter smiled briefly, and shifted the heavy bandolier into a more comfortable position. *How are the mighty fallen . . .* Still, he'd always intended to be first man out on the new planet. Willingly or not, he'd come a long way to see his new home, and it was a moment he didn't intend to share with anyone else. He nodded briefly to the Investigator, and turned round to face the airlock door. Krystel leant over the control panels, and the heavy metal door hissed open. Hunter stepped carefully into the airlock, and the door closed firmly behind him.

The closet-sized airlock was even more claustrophobic than the control deck, but Hunter didn't give a damn. Now that the moment had come to actually face the unknown, he felt suddenly reluctant to go through with it. A familiar panic gnawed at his nerves, threatening to break free. Once the airlock door opened and he stepped outside, he would be face to face with the world he would never leave. While he was on board the pinnace, he could still pretend . . .

The outer door swung open. Thin streamers of mist entered the airlock, bringing the night's chill with them. Hunter raised his chin. Once outside, he'd be the first man ever to set foot on Wolf IV. The history books would know his name. Hunter sniffed. Stuff the history books. He took a deep breath and stepped gingerly out into the new world.

The great hull of the pinnace loomed above him, brilliant in its coat of lights. Mists swirled all around the ship, thick and silver-grey, diffusing the ship's lights before they were swallowed up by the night. Hunter moved slowly away from the airlock, fighting an urge to stick close to the ship for security. The air was bitter cold, and something in it irritated his throat. He coughed several times to clear it. The sound was dull and muted. The ground crunched under his feet, and he knelt down to study it. It was hard to the touch, but cracked and broken from the pinnace's weight. Pumice stone, perhaps; hardened lava from the volcanoes. Hunter shrugged and straightened up again. He knew he should move further away from the ship, but he couldn't quite bring himself to do that yet. The gloom beyond the ship's lights was utterly dark, and intimidating. He let his hands rest on his gunbelt, and activated his comm implant.

"Captain to pinnace. Do you read me?"

"Yes, Captain. Loud and clear." Krystel's calm voice in his ear was infinitely reassuring. "Anything to report?"

"Not a thing. I can't see for any distance, but the area seems deserted. No trace of anything but rock and mists. I'll try again later, when the sun comes up. How long is that?"

"One hour twenty-three minutes. What does it feel like out there, Captain?"

"Cold," said Hunter. "Cold . . . and lonely. I'm coming back in."

He took one last look around. Everything seemed still and silent, but suddenly his hackles rose and his hand dropped to his gun. Nothing had changed, but in that instant Hunter knew without a shadow of a doubt that there was something out there in the night, watching him. There couldn't be. The sensors and the esper had assured him the area was deserted. Hunter trusted both of them implicitly, yet all of his instincts told him he was being watched. He licked his dry lips, and then deliberately turned his back on the darkness. It was nerves, that was all. Just nerves. He stepped back into the airlock, and the door swung shut behind him.

Dawn rose unhurriedly above the featureless horizon, tinting the remaining mists an unhealthy yellow. The mists had begun to disappear the moment the sun showed itself, and the last stubborn remnants were now slowly fading away to nothing. The silver sun was painfully bright and cast sharp-edged shadows. Everything seemed unusually distinct, though everywhere the natural colors were muted and faded by the intensity of the light. The sky was pale green in colour, apparently from dust clouds high up in the atmosphere. The pinnace stood alone on the open ground, a gleaming silver needle on the cracked and broken plain. There was a dark smudge on the horizon, which the ship's probes had identified as a forest. It was too far away to show up in any detail on the pinnace's sensors.

The ship's airlock stood open, with the two marines standing guard beside it. In reality, the ship's sensors would sound a warning long before either man could spot a threat, but the Captain didn't believe in his men sitting around idle. The marines didn't mind, much. The open plain was far more interesting than the cramped confines of the pinnace. Not far away, Dr. Williams was prising free some samples of the crumbling ground and dropping them into a specimen bag. All three men worked hard at seeming calm and at ease, but each of them had a barely suppressed air of jumpiness that showed itself in abrupt, sudden movements.

Russel Corbie leaned against the pinnace hull and wondered how long it would be till the next meal. Breakfast had been one protein cube and a glass of distilled water, neither of which you'd call filling. He'd eaten better in the military prison. He looked around him, but there was still nothing much to see. The open plain was bleak and barren and eerily silent. Corbie smiled sourly. On the way down, his heart had hammered frantically at the thought of the horrible creatures that might be lying in wait for him here, but so far his first day on Wolf IV had been unrelievedly boring. Still, he wasn't exactly unhappy. Given the choice between boredom and hideous monsters, he'd go for the tedium any day.

Corbie was a small, solidly built man in his mid-twenties. His sharp-edged features and dull black uniform gave him an uncanny resemblance to the bird of prey he was named after. His face was habitually dour, and his eyes were wary. His uniform was dirty and sloppy, and looked like several people had slept in it.

There's one like Corbie in every outfit. He knows everyone, has contacts everywhere, and can get you anything. For a price. The Empire doesn't care for such people. Corbie had been in a military prison and resigned to staying there for some time, when the chance came to volunteer for the Hell Squads. At the time, it had seemed like a good idea.

Sven Lindholm was a complete contrast to Corbie. He was tall and muscular, in his mid-thirties, with broad shoulders and an intimidatingly flat stomach. His uniform was perfectly cut and immaculate. His pale blue eyes and short corn-yellow hair gave him a calm, sleepy look that fooled nobody. He wore his sword and gun with the casual grace of long acquaintance, and his hands never moved far from either. Lindholm was a fighter, and looked it.

Corbie sighed again, and Lindholm looked at him, amused. "What is it now, Russ?"

"Nothing. Just thinking."

"Something gloomy, no doubt. I've never known anyone with such a talent for finding things to worry about. Look on the bright side, Russ. We've been here almost three hours, and so far absolutely nothing has tried to kill us. This place is deserted; there's not even a bird in the sky."

"Yeah," said Corbie. "Suspicious, that."

"There's no pleasing you, is there?" said Lindholm. "Would you have preferred it if we'd stepped out of the pinnace and found ourselves face to face with something large and obnoxious with hundreds of teeth?"

"I don't know. Maybe. At least we'd have known where we were, then. This place *feels* wrong. You can't tell me you haven't felt it too, Sven. It isn't natural for an open space like this to be so deserted. I mean, it's not like we're in the middle of a desert. You saw the probes' memories; apart from a few extra volcanoes and the odd patch of stormy weather, this world is practically Earth normal. So where the hell is everything? This kind of planet should be swarming with life."

"Will you cut it out?" said Lindholm. "I'm starting to feel nervous now."

"Good," said Corbie. "I'd hate to feel this worried on my own." He stared at the ground thoughtfully, and hit it a few times with the heel of his boot. The ground cracked and split apart. "Look at this, Sven. Bone-dry. Sucked clean of every last drop of moisture. Can't be because of the day's heat. The sun's up and it's still bloody freezing." He studied the view again, and scowled unhappily. "I don't know; I wasn't expecting a garden planet, but this place gives me the creeps."

"I shouldn't worry about it," said Lindholm. "You'll get used to it, as the years go by."

"You're a real comfort, Sven."

"What are friends for?"

They stood together in silence for a while, studying the featureless plain. The sound of Dr. Williams digging came clearly to them on the quiet.

"What do you think of our Captain?" said Lindholm, as much to keep Corbie from brooding as anything. He already had his own opinion of the Captain.

Corbie's scowl deepened. "All the Captains we could have got, and we had to end up with Scott Hunter. I did a little research on him before we left the *Devastation*. The man is hardworking, a bit of a martinet, and too damned honest for everyone's good. Volunteered for patrol duty out in the Rim worlds, and distinguished himself in four major battles. Could have made Admiral eventually, if he hadn't screwed up. Always assuming he could have learned to keep his opinions to himself, and kiss the right butts."

Lindholm nodded slowly. "We could have done worse."

"Are you kidding?" Corbie shook his head dolefully. "I know his sort. Honest, courageous, and a bloody hero to boot, I'll bet. You can't trust heroes. They'll get you killed one way or another, chasing after their bloody ideals."

"You're a fine one to talk," said Lindholm. "I was there the time you led that charge against the Blood Runners, out in the Obeah Systems, remember?"

Corbie shrugged. "I was drunk."

"Well, you shouldn't have that problem here. The nearest bar is light-years away."

"Don't remind me. I'll have to put some thought into building a still."

"We could have drawn a worse hand," said Lindholm. "It's a dismal-looking place, no doubt about it, but at least it's not another Grendel or Shub."

"As far as we know," said Corbie darkly.

"Cut it out, Russ." Lindholm glanced over at Dr. Williams, and lowered his voice. "What do you know about the rest of our Squad? The way I heard it, the esper got caught making a run for the rebel planet, Mistworld, but I couldn't find out a thing about the doctor, or the Investigator."

"Don't look at me," said Corbie. "I've never even met an Investigator before. I don't normally travel in such high company. The esper's no one special, as far as I know. Just happened to be in the wrong place at the wrong time, and trusted the wrong man. Not bad-looking, though, in a spooky kind of way."

Lindholm snorted. "Forget it, Russ. The Captain won't stand for any tomfoolery. Beats me how you can think about sex at a time like this, anyway."

Corbie shrugged. "I have a reputation to live down to."

"What about the doctor?" said Lindholm. "Why is he here?"

"Ah, the good doctor; a mystery man indeed . . ."

"All right," said Lindholm patiently. "What have you heard?"

"Nothing definite, but the word was that he was involved in some kind of scandal to do with the adjusted men. Forbidden augmentations, that sort of thing."

Lindholm whistled softly. "If that's the case, he's lucky to be alive. The Empire's been really tight over that kind of thing since the Hadenman rebellion."

"Right. Those killer cyborgs threw a scare into everyone. Anyway, as I understand it, Williams was given a straight choice: volunteer for the Hell Squads or end up as spare parts in a body bank."

"And I was thinking we were lucky to have a doctor in the Squad," said Lindholm. "Still, it could have been worse. He could have been a clonelegger."

"Will you stop saying it could have been worse! It's bad enough as it is. All the Squads I could have been in, and what do I end up with: Captain Pureheart, a Mad Doctor, and a flaming Investigator. I don't even want to think what she did to end up here. Those people are as inhuman as the things they kill."

"At least she's on our side," said Lindholm.

Corbie looked at him. "Investigators aren't on anybody's side."

The pinnace control deck looked even gloomier than usual with the control panels dead. The single overhead light only showed up the darkness of the shadows. Captain Hunter and Investigator Krystel lay still in their crash webbings, and their eyes saw only light. Patched into the onboard computers through their comm implants, the probes' recordings filled their eyes and ears to the exclusion of the real world.

Hunter concentrated on the scene before him. With direct input, it was only too easy to become lost in the sound and fury of the probes' memories and forget the real world and its imperatives. He fast-forwarded relentlessly, pausing only when the computers pointed out scenes of importance or possible significance. He felt guilty at leaving the real work to the computers, but he needed an overview of the situation as quickly as possible. There were decisions he had to make, and they were already starting to pile up. When he had a chance he'd study the records in real time, weighing and evaluating every detail, but right now all he wanted was information on possible threats and dangers. Everything else could wait. Scene after scene flashed before his eyes, and Hunter's scowl deepened as Wolf IV reluctantly gave up its secrets.

In the north, volcanoes threw molten fire into the sky. The lava burned a deep and sullen red, and ashes fell like rain. There were vast plains of cooling ash, and all around the land was baked dry and brittle. A planet as old as Wolf IV was supposed to be should have left its volcanic stage behind centuries ago, but instead a long chain of smoking volcanoes studded the north of the single great continent, like so many warning balefires.

The oceans were racked by endless storms, and among the mountainous, churning waves, huge creatures fought a never-ending battle for survival. It was difficult to judge their exact size from a distance, even seen against the height of the waves, but the sheer ponderousness of the creatures' movements hinted at appallingly vast dimensions. Hunter didn't even want to think what the damned things would weigh on land. It was clear that in the future all travelling would have to be by land and air; no ship would survive an ocean voyage. Some of the creatures rending and tearing each other looked to be almost as big as the *Devastation*.

Huge areas of forest filled the centre of the continent; solid masses of dirty yellow vegetation. The probes didn't show much in the way of detail, but trees were usually a good sign for a colonist. You could do a lot with wood. Hunter smiled for the first time as the probes' memories moved on to show him large areas of open grassland in the south. Even so, he kept a firm grip on his enthusiasm. First rule of the Hell Squads: never take anything for granted. On an alien world, nothing is necessarily what it seems. All right, from a distance it looked like ordinary, everyday grass, although the colour was a bit vile. But on Scarab, the long grass had turned out to be carnivorous. On Loki, the grass had an acid-based sap and spread like plague in the night. Everything on a new planet had to be treated as potentially dangerous, until proved otherwise by exhaustive testing. And then the scene changed again as a new probe's memories patched in, and Hunter's heart missed a beat. He hit the freeze frame, fixing the image in place, and swallowed with a suddenly dry throat.

"Investigator," he said finally through his comm implant, "Patch into probe seven. I've found something."

There were structures of stone and glass and gleaming metal. Jagged-edged turrets erupted from asymmetrical buildings. Strange lights blazed in the windows of huge stone monoliths. Low domes glimmered with pearl-like translucency. In the centre of everything, a spiked tower of gleaming copper reached up to touch the sky. And everywhere, hanging lightly between the oppressive shapes and buildings, were frothy strands of gossamer walkways.

"It's a city," said Hunter, his voice awed and hushed.

"Looks like it," said Krystel. "Roughly circular, four miles in diameter. No signs of life forms as yet."

"I've got the computers checking for similar sightings."

"They won't find any. We're pretty much near the end of the recordings. If there were any other cities like this, we'd have come across them long before now."

"Switch to the viewscreen," said Hunter. "I want full computer analysis of the recording. This has top priority until I tell you otherwise."

"Aye, Captain."

The alien city disappeared from Hunter's eyes, and the control deck reappeared around him. After the haunting, mysterious views of the city, the Spartan Empire fittings had a comforting familiarity. The Investigator was already bent over the control panels, calling up more data. Hunter leaned back carefully in his webbing, and studied the alien city on the viewscreen. Now that the first flush of excitement had died down, he found that his skin was crawling, and he had to keep fighting down an urge to look away. The shapes of the structures were ugly, twisted . . . *wrong*, somehow. They made no sense. There was something actually unnerving about the alien shapes and angles. Whatever theories of architecture had produced the city, they followed no human patterns of logic or aesthetics.

"How far away from us is it?" he asked, and was relieved to note that his voice sounded somewhat calmer.

"Fourteen, fifteen miles. Walking distance. We could be there in a day."

Hunter looked sideways at Krystel, but didn't say anything. She might see fifteen miles as walking distance, but he sure as hell didn't. Fifteen miles? He scowled unhappily. He hadn't walked that far since Basic Training. And he'd hated it then. He shrugged, and turned his attention back to the viewscreen. Something about the alien city nagged at him. It only took him a moment to realise what. The labyrinth of twisting streets appeared to be completely empty. Nothing moved in the city. Hunter studied the viewscreen for a long time, and then activated his comm implant.

"Esper DeChance, this is the Captain. Please join me on the control deck immediately."

"Aye, Captain. On my way."

Hunter shut down his comm unit, and looked at the Investigator. "No life, no movement. Nobody's home. What do you make of it?"

"Too early to tell, Captain." Krystel drew a slender, villainous-looking cigar from her sleeve pocket, and took her time about lighting it. "The city could be deserted for any number of reasons, few of them good. And anything alien is always potentially dangerous." She looked at Hunter. "Strictly speaking, we ought to report this immediately to the Empire."

"But if we do that," said Hunter, "we'll have to wait till they send in an official Investigatory team. And that could mean a long delay before they send us any colonists . . . or the extra equipment that comes with the colonists. And we need that equipment."

"Yes," said Krystel. "There is that. There's only one choice open to us, Captain. We need more information, so we're going to have to go there and take a look for ourselves. We need to know what happened to the city's inhabitants, and why. If there's anything on this planet deadly enough to wipe out an entire city's population, we'd better find out all we can about it, before it comes looking for us."

"I couldn't agree more," said Hunter. "That's why I've sent for the esper."

Krystel sniffed, and studied the glowing end of her cigar. "Telepathic evidence is subjective, and therefore unreliable."

"Espers have their uses. And I'll trust a human mind over a computer any day."

The door behind them hissed open, and the esper Megan DeChance stepped onto the control deck. She was a short, wraithlike woman in her late thirties, with long silver-blond hair. Her eyes were green and very steady, and like the rest of her face, gave nothing at all away. She nodded once to Hunter and ignored the Investigator. Hunter's heart sank. Traditionally, espers and Investigators didn't get along. By virtue of their telepathy and empathy, espers tended to be fanatically pro-life. Investigators weren't.

"Right, esper," said Hunter briskly. "I want a full scan of the immediate area, twenty-mile radius. Never mind plant or animal life; I'm interested in intelligent life forms."

DeChance raised an eyebrow but said nothing. She sat cross-legged on the deck between the two webbings, arranged herself comfortably, and closed her eyes. She sent her thoughts up and out, and her mind spread across the world like ripples on a pond. The Hell Squad were bright sparks in and around the pinnace. Everywhere else was dark. She spread out further, and the world blossomed before her. Lives shone in the darkness like flaring torches and guttering candles, but none of them burned with the steady intensity of the intelligent mind.

And yet there was something strange, right on the edge of her perception. Its light was strong but muted, and curiously indistinct. DeChance studied it warily. In a slow, creeping way it seemed to be aware of her. The esper started to back away, but even as she broke the contact, the light suddenly flared up into an awful brilliance. It burned in hideous colours, and it knew where she was. DeChance pulled the darkness around her like a cloak. Something new was abroad in the night, something huge and powerful. There were other things in the darkness too, and one by one they were waking up. Their lights grew bright and awful, and DeChance pulled back her esp, folding it in upon itself, and locking it safely away inside her mind again. She opened her eyes, and looked shakily at Captain Hunter.

"There's something out there, Captain. It's not like anything I've ever encountered before. It's big, very old, and very powerful."

"Dangerous?" said the Investigator.

"I don't know," said DeChance. "Probably. And it's not alone."

For a long moment, nobody said anything. Hunter felt a chill run up his spine as he realised just how shaken the esper was.

"All right," he said finally. "Thank you, esper; that will be all. Please join the others outside. We'll be out shortly. Dismissed."

DeChance nodded and left. Hunter and Krystel looked at each other.

"It has to be the city," said Krystel. "We've got to go there, Captain."

"Yes. You've more . . . experience with aliens than I have, Investigator. Assuming we do find something there, what's the best procedure?"

Krystel grinned around her cigar. "Find it. Trap it. Kill it. And burn the body afterwards, just to be sure."

Dr. Williams sat quietly in the shadow of the pinnace, hugging his knees to his chest and staring out at his new world. All in all it looked decidedly bleak and barren, and the endless quiet was getting on his nerves. Still, he was lucky to be in the Hell Squad, and he knew it. If the Empire had been able to prove half the charges they'd made against him . . . but they hadn't. His money and influence had seen to that. For a time.

He thought he'd get away with a few years' confinement in some comfortable open prison, or perhaps just a fine and a public admonition. But in the end, too many people decided they couldn't risk the truth coming out at a trial. So they pulled a few strings, and Dr. Williams found himself heading out towards the edge of the Empire and some nice anonymous Hell Squad planet, where his secrets could be buried with him.

It had all been very neatly done. Men he'd trusted for years had betrayed him, under the pressure of massive bribes and death threats, and suddenly he'd stood alone. He could either go with the Hell Squad or be shot in the back while trying to escape. Williams had screamed and raged and threatened, but little good it had done him. He hugged his knees tightly and glared out over the open plain.

Graham Williams was a tall, slender, handsome man in his late fifties, who looked thirty years younger. His skin was fresh and glowing, and his thick curly hair was jet-black. He had a doctor's warm, professional smile and a pleasant manner. Half his organs, most of his skin, and all of his hair had come from other people. The donors had all

been anonymous, of course. Body snatchers rarely bother
to learn the names of their victims.

Williams also had a great many personal augmentations
that the Empire hadn't found out about in the short time
they'd held him. Unfortunately, they were only of limited
use to him now. The implanted energy crystals that ran
the devices had strictly limited life spans. Once they were
drained of power, all the high tech in his body would be
just so much useless junk. He'd have to make the crystals
last until he could acquire some more.

He smiled suddenly. That was in the future. For the
moment, though the others might not realise it, he was
the most powerful man in the Squad. Let the Captain
enjoy his moment in charge. He'd find out the truth soon
enough. Williams' smile widened as retractable steel claws
appeared at the fingertips of his right hand and then disappeared again.

He looked down at the soil samples he'd gathered, lying
in a neat row in their little bags, spread out on the ground
before him. He'd taken the samples as much to keep busy
as anything, but you never knew your luck. There were
often riches to be found in the soil, for those who knew
where to look. There was money to be made on this planet
somewhere, and he had no intention of missing out on any
of it. The pinnace's diagnostic equipment was primitive, to
say the least, but it would do the job. Williams frowned,
and hugged his knees a little tighter. It wasn't at all what
he was used to. His surgery had been known throughout
the Empire; said by many to be the greatest since the
fabled laboratories of lost Haden itself. All gone now, of
course. Destroyed, by him, so that its secrets couldn't be
used against him.

After the rebellion of the cyborg Hadenmen, the Empire
had banned most forms of human augmentation. But there
were always those willing to pay highly for forbidden
delights. Most of the banned devices had been fairly harmless anyway, as long as they were used sensibly. With
restraint. He'd just provided a service, that was all. If he
hadn't done it, someone else would have. All right, some

of his patients had died, on the table and afterwards. But they knew the risks when they came to him. And most had lived, and lived well, through the extra senses and devices he'd given them.

They all came to him; the rich, the titled, the jaded, and the decadent. All those with hidden needs and darker appetites. And to each he gave what they asked for, and charged accordingly. His prices were high, but they could afford it. Besides, he had his own needs, too.

It was the Empire's fault he'd become what he was. He'd made his name and his reputation with his work on the Wampyr, the adjusted men. They were to have been the Empire's new shock troops, strong and awful and ruthlessly efficient, but someone High Up got scared of their potential, and the Empress herself closed the project down. Williams had refused to give up his life's work. He went underground, and he went private. And his triumphs with the Wampyr were nothing to what he might have achieved if the Empire hadn't caught up with him.

He should never have relied so much on the body snatchers.

But that was all behind him now. He had a new life and new opportunities. Doctors were always in short supply on colony worlds. One way or another, he would become a man of wealth and standing again. And some way, somehow, he'd use that wealth and power to get off this stinking dirtball and back into the Empire. And then they'd pay. Then they'd all pay, for what they'd done to him.

Outside the airlock, Corbie glared at Megan DeChance.

"A city? An alien city? I don't believe it. I just don't bloody believe it! All the planets the Empire had to choose from and they had to drop us on a world that's already inhabited! I mean, don't they check for things like that first?"

"No," said Lindholm. "That's our job. It may not turn out too badly, Russ. There's a lot that aliens could teach us about this planet, things we need to know. I'm willing to be friendly if they are."

"It's not very likely, Sven," said Corbie. "You know the Empire's attitude to aliens. They get put in their place, or they get put in the ground. No other choice available."

"This is a new world," said Lindholm. "Things could be different here."

Corbie sniffed. "Try telling that to the Investigator."

"I'm afraid it's not that simple," said DeChance quietly. "According to the probes, there aren't any other cities. And this one appears to be deserted."

"Wait a minute," said Corbie. "You mean there's nobody there?"

"There's something there," said DeChance. "I felt its presence."

The two marines waited for her to continue, and then realised she'd said all she was going to. Corbie kicked disgustedly at the ground.

"Mysteries. I hate bloody mysteries."

"I doubt it's anything we can't handle."

The marines looked round sharply as Williams came over to join them. He smiled at them warmly, and nodded to the esper.

"I'm sorry if I interrupted you. I didn't mean to intrude . . ."

"No, that's all right, Doc," said Lindholm. "This concerns you as well. Seems there's an abandoned alien city not far from where we've parked."

"Fascinating," said Williams. "I do hope we're going to explore it."

"Great," muttered Corbie. "Another bloody hero."

Williams ignored him and concentrated his charm on Lindholm and the esper. "What do you make of our new home, my friends?"

"A little on the desolate side," said Lindholm. "I've seen livelier cemeteries."

"It's not very attractive, I'll admit," said Williams calmly. "But I wouldn't write it off just yet. There may be hidden virtues. Geology isn't my strong suit, but if I've read the signs correctly, the ship's computers just might find these soil samples very interesting."

He patted the satchel he was carrying. Corbie looked at him with new interest.

"Are you saying there might be something here worth digging for? Gold, precious stones; things like that?"

"That sort of thing, yes," said Williams. "I think a few test drillings might well turn up something to our mutual advantage."

"Jewels are fine," said Lindholm. "But you can't eat them. For a long time to come, our only interest in the soil is going to be how well it supports our crops. The ship's rations will run out in a few months, and that's if we're careful. After that, we're on our own. Presumably there are plants and animals here somewhere that will prove safe to eat, but we'll always need our own crops to supply us with vitamins and trace elements. First things first, Doctor."

"You've been studying up on this," said Corbie.

"I thought one of us should," said Lindholm.

"I shouldn't worry too much about the crops," said Williams. "The volcanoes might look rather dramatic, but they help to produce good soil. All that pumice stone is full of phosphates, lime, and potash. Just add the right nitrates, and food should come leaping up out of the ground in no time."

"Unfortunately, there are complications," said DeChance. "Have you come across any signs of life yet, Doctor?"

"No," said Williams. "Is that significant?"

"Wouldn't surprise me," said Corbie darkly.

"Don't mind him," said Lindholm. "He thinks they're all hiding from him. And if I was an alien getting my first glimpse of Corbie, I'd think about hiding too."

"I'm surprised the Captain hasn't joined us yet," said Williams casually. "I thought he'd be eager to set about taking in his new territory. That *is* what military types like to do, after all. Or do we have a Captain who doesn't like to get his hands dirty?"

"He seems solid enough," said Lindholm, frowning.

"And he can take all the time he likes about coming out, as far as I'm concerned," said Corbie. "It's nice and peaceful out here without him. Who needs some officer type yelling orders? That's one of the few good things about being in a Hell Squad; no more dumb rules and regulations."

"The Captain's in charge of the Squad," said Williams. "He still gives the orders."

"Yeah, but that's different," said Corbie. "What I'm talking about is no more having to salute, no more surprise inspections; no standing guard in the rain because your boots aren't shiny enough, or slaving all day over make-work designed to keep the lower orders busy. I've had a bellyful of that in my time. And besides . . . just suppose I did decide I wasn't going to obey an order; what could Hunter do about it? There aren't any Guards or Military Police here to back him up. There's just him. . . ."

"Wrong," said Investigator Krystel.

They all looked round quickly, to discover Krystel and Captain Hunter standing just outside the open airlock. Corbie couldn't help noticing they both had hands resting near their disrupters. He smiled uneasily, and stood very still.

"The Captain is in command here," said Krystel. "You do as he says, or I'll hurt you, marine. We're still citizens of the Empire, with all the responsibilities that entails."

"Oh sure," said Corbie quickly. "Anything you say, Investigator."

"I gather some of you are interested in mineral rights," said Hunter. "Jewels, precious metals, and the like. If I were you, I should bear in mind that very few colonists ever strike it rich. They're too busy working every hour God sends just to keep their heads above water. No, people; it's much more likely you'll get yourself killed doing something stupid, because you were daydreaming about gold mines instead of keeping your mind on the job. For the time being, just concentrate on keeping yourself and the rest of the Squad alive. Now then, since you've all had a nice little rest, I think it's time for a spot of healthy exercise. Some fifteen miles from here is a deserted alien city. We're going to go and take a look at it. On foot, with full field kit and standard backpacks. We start in thirty minutes."

"On foot?" said Williams. "Why not fly there in the pinnace? There's more than enough power in the batteries."

"That's right, there is," said Hunter. "And that's where it's staying, until we have an emergency that justifies using it. I'm certainly not wasting it on a joy ride. Besides, I think it's better that we take our time approaching the city. This world is still new to us; if we're going to make mistakes, let's make them where it doesn't matter. Oh, and people, keep your eyes open and your heads down. This is a reconnaissance mission, not an attack force."

"But what about the pinnace itself?" asked Williams. "Is it wise to just go off and leave it unguarded? Anything could happen to it while we were gone. And if anything were to happen to the equipment stored on board . . ."

"Dr. Williams," said Hunter pleasantly, "that's enough. I'm the Captain; I don't have to explain myself to you. And I don't take kindly to having my orders questioned all the time. You must learn to trust me, Doctor, and obey my orders implicitly. Because if you don't, I'll let the Investigator have you. The pinnace will be perfectly safe in our absence. Isn't that right, Investigator?"

"Right," said Krystel indistinctly, relighting her cigar. She puffed at it a few times to make sure she'd got it just the way she wanted, then fixed Williams with a cold stare. "We'll activate the force screen before we go, and the computers will be on battle readiness until we return. All told, the ship will probably be safer than we will."

"You got that right," said Corbie. "If we're going up against aliens, I want hazard pay."

"Technically speaking, we shouldn't really call them aliens," said Dr. Williams. "This is their world, after all. If anyone's alien here, it's us."

The Investigator chuckled quietly. "Wrong, Doctor. Aliens are aliens, no matter where you find them."

"And the only good alien is a dead alien," said Corbie. "Right, Investigator?"

Krystel smiled. "Right, marine."

"How can you justify that?" said DeChance heatedly. "Everything that lives has some common ground. We share the same thoughts, the same feelings, the same hopes and needs. . . ."

"You ever met an alien?" asked Krystel.

"No, but . . ."

"Not many have." Krystel drew on her cigar, blew a perfect smoke ring, and stared at it for a long moment. "Alien isn't just a noun, esper; it's an adjective. Alien; as in strange, different, inhuman. Unnatural. There's no room for the alien inside the Empire, and this planet's been a part of the Empire from the moment an Imperial ship discovered it. That's Empire law."

"It doesn't have to be that way here," said Lindholm slowly. "If we could contact the aliens peacefully, make some kind of alliance . . ."

"The Empire would find out eventually," said Hunter. "And then they'd put a stop to it."

"But why?" said DeChance. "Why would they care?"

"Because aliens represent the unknown," said Corbie. "And the Empire's afraid of the unknown. Simple as that. Not too surprising, really. The unknown is always threatening to those in power."

"Sometimes they have reason to be afraid," said Krystel. "I was there on Grendel, when the Sleepers awoke."

For a long time no one said anything.

"I thought no one got out of there alive," said Lindholm finally.

Krystel smiled humourlessly. "I was lucky."

"I think that's enough chatting for one day," said Hunter. "Get your gear together, people. Keep it simple, the bare minimum. Remember, you've got to carry it, and we might have to travel in a hurry. Report back here in thirty minutes, ready to leave. Don't be late, or we'll go without you. Now move it."

The Squad turned as one and filed quickly back into the pinnace. At the rear, hanging back, Corbie looked at Lindholm.

"An alien city," he said quietly. "You ever seen an alien, Sven?"

"Can't say I have," said Lindholm. "That's what Investigators are for. I met a Wampyr once, on Golgotha. He was pretty strange, but not actually alien. How about you? You ever met an alien?"

"Not yet." Corbie frowned unhappily. "I just hope our Investigator has enough sense not to get us in over our heads. We're a long way from help."

CHAPTER TWO

In the Forest of the Night

THE silver sun rode high on the pale green sky. The world lay stark and bare under the brilliant light, and no sound broke the silence. The mists were gone, dispersed by the rising sun, but the day was no warmer. The Hell Squad moved warily through the quiet morning, walking in single file, their hands never far from their gunbelts. Hunter led the way, alert for any sign of movement on the open plain, but for as far as he could see there wasn't a trace of life anywhere. There were no animals, no birds in the sky, not even an insect. The continuing silence was eerie and disquieting. The soft sound of the Squad's boots on the plain was quickly swallowed up by the quiet, and there wasn't even a murmur of wind.

Hunter hefted his backpack into a slightly more comfortable position and tried not to think about the miles of hard open ground that lay between him and the alien city. His legs ached, his back was killing him, and there was still another nine, ten miles to go. And what was worse, his feeling of being watched was back again. He'd been free of it for a while, but once they'd left the pinnace behind, the feeling had come back even stronger. Hunter scowled. He'd never felt this worried before, not even when he was heading into battle. Not even during the bad times; the times he'd panicked for no good reason. He swallowed hard. He felt light-headed and his hands were shaking. He could feel the beginnings of panic stirring within him.

Not now. Please, not now!

He fought the panic fiercely, refusing to give in to it, and slowly it subsided again. Hunter breathed more easily, but he wasn't fooled. He knew it would be back again, the moment he weakened. Hairs prickled on the back of his neck. The feeling of being watched was as strong as ever. Hunter kept wanting to stop and look around him, but he didn't. He didn't want to look jumpy in front of the others.

He raised his hands to his mouth and blew on them. The morning was several hours old, but it was still barely above freezing. Hunter rubbed his hands together, wishing the Empire had included winter clothing in its list of essential supplies. The heating elements in his uniform could only do so much. Right now he'd have traded his disrupter for a good pair of thick gloves.

The forest drew slowly closer, and Hunter studied it dispassionately. It looked as if they were nearly upon it, but distances were deceiving in the overbright light. They'd been approaching the forest boundary for the best part of an hour, but only now was it starting to give up its secrets. Hunter frowned. What little he could make out wasn't exactly encouraging. The huge trees were packed close together and soared up into the sky. The wide trunks were iron-black, gnarled and whorled, and the foliage was a dark, bitter yellow. The leaves were all different shapes and sizes, and the twisted branches drooped down to the ground as often as not.

The ground approaching the forest was cracked and broken, and clumps of spiky grass sprouted up from the crevices. The grass grew thicker and more abundant as the Squad finally drew near the forest boundary, some of it rising to almost two feet in places. Hunter called a halt so that Williams could take a close look at it. The doctor knelt down and studied a clump of grass carefully without touching it. The long spikes were wide and flat, pale violet in color, and marked with a curious ribbing, almost like bones.

"Interesting," said Williams. "The grass is purple but the leaves on the trees are yellow. Vegetation is usually all the same color, particularly when it's growing under the same conditions."

"Maybe they draw their nourishment from different sources," suggested Hunter.

"Perhaps," said Williams. "I'll take a few specimens and run them through the computers later."

Hunter looked at the Investigator, who shrugged. "No objections, Captain. We've all had the standard immunization shots."

"All right," said Hunter. "Take your time, Doctor. I'm sure we could all use a little rest."

"Certainly," said Williams. He looked at Corbie. "Pull me up a handful of grass, young man, while I prepare a specimen bag to hold it."

Corbie shrugged, and knelt down beside the nearest clump of grass. He grabbed a handful, and then gasped and let go quickly.

"What is it?" asked Krystel.

Corbie opened his hand and stared at it. Long cuts marked his palm and the insides of his fingers. Blood welled from his hand and dripped onto the thirsty ground. He reached into his pocket with his free hand, pulled out a grimy handkerchief, and pressed it gingerly against the cuts, then straightened up and glared at Williams, more angry than hurt. "The edges of the grass are razor-sharp! I could have lost my fingers!"

"Now, that is interesting," said Krystel.

Corbie looked at her. He said nothing, but his gaze spoke volumes.

"All right," said Hunter quickly. "Let that be a warning to all of us. From now on, keep your hands to yourselves and don't touch anything until we're sure it's safe. And Corbie, use your first aid kit. That rag you've got there is filthy, and I don't want your cuts getting infected.

Corbie sniffed and looked put upon, but accepted Lindholm's offer of a clean bandage and wrapped it carefully round his cuts. Lindholm knelt down and cut away a few spikes of grass with his dagger. Williams slipped them into a self-sealing bag and tucked it carefully into his backpack. Hunter checked that everyone was ready, and then led his Squad on towards the waiting forest. He wasn't too unhappy about the incident. Corbie hadn't been badly hurt, and it was a lesson his people needed to learn. Apart from the Investigator, they hadn't been showing nearly enough respect for their new environment. Even now, it might take a serious accident before they did, and he couldn't afford to lose anybody.

The forest spread out across the horizon as they approached its boundary. It was bigger than Hunter had expected, and looked to be several miles wide. He activated his comm implant and patched into the pinnace's computers. Three point seven miles at its widest, to be exact. Hunter frowned suddenly as he shut down his implant. He shouldn't really be using the implant for this sort of thing. Once the energy crystals in his body were depleted, all his high-tech implants would be useless. Better to save his tech for when it was needed. As he made a mental note to mention it to the others, the Investigator came to a sudden halt beside him. He turned to her enquiringly while the rest of the Squad pulled up around them. Krystel was looking intently at the ground just ahead.

"Everyone stay where they are," she said softly. "Captain, I suggest we all draw our guns."

"Do it," said Hunter. There was a brief whisper of sound as the Squad's disrupters left their holsters. Hunter glanced unobtrusively about him, but couldn't see anything threatening. "What is it, Investigator?"

"Straight ahead, Captain; two o'clock. I don't know what it is, but it's moving."

Hunter looked where she'd indicated, and a chill went through him that had nothing to do with the morning cold. Something long and spiny was oozing up out of one of the cracks in the ground. It was flat and thin, and the same dirty yellow as the foliage on the trees. At first, Hunter thought it was some kind of jointed worm or centipede, but the more he looked at it, the more it resembled a long strand of creeper or ivy. It had no visible eyes or mouth, but the raised end swayed back and forth as though testing the air. It was as wide as a man's hand, and already several feet long, though more of it was still emerging from the crack.

Dozens of hair-fine legs suddenly appeared at its sides and flexed impatiently as the rest of the long body snapped up out of the crevice. The creature scuttled across the open ground with horrible speed and then froze in place, the front end slightly lifted, as though listening.

"Ugly-looking thing," said Corbie, trying to keep his voice light, and failing. "Look at the size of it. Is it a plant or an animal?"

"Could be both, or neither," said the Investigator. Her gun was trained on the creature and had been since it appeared. "Would you like it as a specimen, Dr. Williams?"

"Don't think I've got a bag big enough to carry it in, thank you," said Williams.

"Kill it," said Corbie. "I'm not sharing the pinnace with that horrible thing."

"Take it easy," said Hunter. "We don't know that it's dangerous, and it *is* the first living creature we've come across. It could tell us a lot about this world."

"I don't think it's got anything to say that I'd want to hear," Corbie replied.

"There are more of them," said DeChance suddenly. The esper had one hand pressed to her forehead, and her eyes were closed. "They're right here with us, just under the surface. They're moving back and forth in the earth. I think they were attracted by the sound of our approach."

"Can you read them?" asked Hunter quietly.

"No. They're too different, Captain. Too alien. The few impressions I'm getting don't make any sense at all."

She broke off as more of the creatures suddenly thrust up through the cracks in the ground. Within moments there were dozens of the things all around, curling and coiling and scuttling back and forth. They moved in quick little darts and flurries, crawling over and under each other without pausing. The Squad formed a defensive circle, guns at the ready. Corbie gripped his disrupter tightly, and wished the Captain would give the order to open fire. The damned things moved too quickly for his liking. He had an uneasy suspicion they could move even quicker if they wanted to. Probably even as fast as a running man . . .

"Orders, Captain?" asked Lindholm, his voice calm and controlled as always.

"Stand your ground," said Hunter. "They don't seem too interested in us. I think we can afford to practise live and let live with anything that seems willing to leave us alone. There's an opening to the left. Start moving towards it."

He stepped forward to lead the way, and every one of the creatures snapped round to point in his direction. Hunter froze where he was. The creatures held their position, their raised front ends swaying slightly.

"They respond to movement, Captain," said the Investigator. "And I don't think they believe in live and let live."

"Wait a minute," Corbie put in. "Look at the heads. Those are mouths, aren't they? I would have sworn they didn't have mouths a minute ago."

"They've got teeth as well," said Lindholm. "And I'm sure they didn't have those before. What the hell is going on here?"

"Watch it!" said DeChance. "They're moving!"

The creatures surged forward with unnerving speed. Krystel took careful aim with her disrupter and blew a hole through the middle of the pack. The rest of the Squad followed her lead, and the air was full of the hiss of energy bolts. Half the creatures disappeared instantly, vaporized by the searing energy. More were torn apart by the shock waves, and ragged lengths of dirty yellow flew through the air, still coiling and twitching. The survivors slithered back into the cracks in the ground and were gone in seconds. Krystel holstered her gun and drew her sword, then moved cautiously forward. Hunter accompanied her, wrinkling his nose as the smell hit him. Both the dead and the injured creatures were already decaying, falling apart and melting into a stinking grey jelly. Krystel stirred some of the bodies with the tip of her sword, but there was no reaction.

"If all the plants are this active, the forest should prove positively lively." Krystel paused and looked at Hunter. "Captain, I strongly suggest we stay clear of the forest. We don't have enough information to judge the risks accurately. There could be anything at all in there just waiting for us to come within reach."

Hunter scowled. Theoretically, she was right. But going around the forest instead of through it would add hours to their journey. It would also mean having to spend at least one night out in the open—all alone, unprotected, in the dark. . . .

"We're going into the forest, Investigator. Our disrupters took care of those plant creatures easily enough. Listen up, people! We're going to enter the forest in single file. Stay close, but no bunching up. Don't touch anything and keep your eyes open. Guns at the ready at all times, but don't fire unless you've got something specific to aim at. Now follow me."

He led the way into the trees, and the forest gloom closed in around him. The overhead canopy of branches let through some light, but even so, it was like walking straight from day into twilight. The others followed him in, giving the scorched remains on the ground a wide berth. Hunter stopped a few yards inside the boundary, and the Squad stood together a moment, getting the feel of the forest. It felt a little warmer among the trees, but it wasn't a comfortable warmth—it was the humid warmth of illness and decay. There was a faint, unpleasant odour on the air, and the crowding trees were distinctly claustrophobic.

Krystel checked that her force shield bracelet was primed and ready, and then drew her gun. She still carried her sword in her other hand. Hunter would have liked to check his bracelet as well, but he didn't. It might make him look nervous and indecisive. A Captain had to appear calm and confident at all times, if he was to retain the trust of those under him. He had to appear to know what he was doing, even when he wasn't sure. Especially then. Hunter frowned. He didn't like putting his people at risk by going through the forest, but all the other alternatives were worse. The straightforward logic of that didn't do a thing to ease his conscience. He looked unobtrusively around him to see what the rest of the Squad made of the forest.

The Investigator looked cold and collected, as always. She was staring ahead into the gloom, tapping the flat of her sword lightly against her leg. Dr. Williams was looking cheerfully about, fascinated by the alien trees, smiling again. It wasn't natural for a man to smile as often as he did. The two marines were talking quietly together. Corbie seemed somewhat rattled, but then he always did. Lindholm looked relaxed and at ease. Presumably once you'd survived the Golgotha Arenas, there wasn't much left that could scare you. Megan DeChance's face was blank, and her eyes were miles away. Hunter's mouth thinned. Espers had their uses, but you couldn't trust them. Like Investigators, they weren't really human; not deep down where it counted.

Hunter turned his attention back to the forest. It seemed quiet, almost peaceful. Maybe it was. It didn't make any difference in the long run. He had a job to do, and he was going to do it come what may. Wolf IV was his chance to redeem himself, in his own eyes if not those of the Empire. He'd failed as Captain of a starship because he was weak, allowing his fear to get the better of him. This time he'd do it right, by the book and by the numbers. This time, he wasn't going to fail. Whatever it cost. He moved slowly forward into the forest gloom, and the Squad followed him.

They moved cautiously through the oppressive silence, watching and listening, but there was only the dim light and the soft, muffled sounds of their boots on the forest floor. Hunter looked at Krystel, striding unconcernedly at his shoulder. Did she ever worry about the things normal people worried about? Like failing, making mistakes, being less than the best at what you did? Hunter almost smiled. Krystel was an Investigator, an instrument of death and destruction that just happened to look like a human being. Hunter's brief glow of amusement faded quickly away as he considered the implications of that thought. If the Squad was to survive on Wolf IV, they were going to have to learn to work together, as a team. He wasn't sure if that was possible with Krystel. Or with the esper, for that matter.

Hunter smiled slightly. The Squad was his responsibility; he'd just have to make it possible. He moved a little closer to Krystel so that they could talk quietly without the others hearing.

"Tell me, Investigator. How much actual experience do you have with alien cultures?"

Krystel glanced at him briefly, and then looked back at the forest. "Just the two, Captain. Once on Loki, and then on Grendel."

She didn't say any more. She didn't have to. The aliens on Grendel had turned out to be non-indigenous. They were a genetically engineered killing force, left in suspended animation by their long-departed creators. Whatever they'd been created to fight was also long gone, but when the archeologists woke them up, they woke up mad and they woke up fighting. Their weapons had been interred with them; high tech implants that were the equal of any Empire weapon. They were monsters and they were unstoppable. They slaughtered everything sent against them. Luckily, the aliens had no starships of their own. They were trapped on Grendel. In the end the Imperial Fleet moved in and systematically burned off the whole planet from orbit.

And Krystel had been the Investigator assigned to work with the archeologists. The one who'd missed the first signs of danger. No wonder she'd ended up in a Hell Squad.

Hunter was more disturbed by that than he wanted to admit. It stood to reason that any Investigator in a Hell Squad would have to be second-rate, but he'd assumed it would at least be someone who knew their business. . . . He frowned as he realised how much he'd been unconsciously relying on Krystel's knowledge and expertise to help him through the early days on Wolf IV. Now it seemed the burden was going to fall on him alone.

Krystel watched the Captain's face out of the corner of her eye. She could all but read his thoughts in his face. Let him worry; she'd prove him wrong. Prove them all wrong. Anyone would have missed the signs on Grendel. No Investigator had ever encountered such a thing, before or since. It wasn't her fault, no matter what the Empire had said afterwards. She kept a careful watch on the forest around her, but she was more occupied with thoughts of the alien city. She could feel a familiar excitement growing within her. The challenge of the unknown; the chance to take on an alien culture and prove herself superior to it in the only way that mattered: by gun and sword. Krystel smiled inwardly. Do a good enough job on the alien city, and the Empire might even reinstate her. Stranger things had happened.

Megan DeChance walked through the forest with downcast eyes. There was nothing to see, but still she knew that they were not alone. She could feel watching eyes all around them, like a pressure on her skin. She kept her mind firmly closed lest the pressure grow too strong and roll over her like a wave and drown her. She forced herself to lift her head and look about her, but there was only the forest. Tall, twisted trees loomed all around her, dark and glistening in the twilight of an alien sun. Seen up close, the foliage was an unpleasant yellow, like rancid butter. The black bark was knotted and bumpy, and she could have seen strange faces in the shapes if she'd chosen. The trees stood closely together, but drew apart here and there to form the narrow path they were following. DeChance swallowed hard. A path implied that someone or something passed through the forest on a regular basis. Or had done so. It might even lead straight to the city.

"Captain," she said clearly, "I think we should stop a moment."

Hunter raised his hand, and the Squad came to a halt. He looked back at DeChance. "What is it, esper?"

"The path we're following is too regular to be natural, Captain. And I keep getting the feeling we're being watched."

Hunter nodded slowly. "Listen to the forest, esper. Tell me what you hear."

DeChance nodded reluctantly, and her eyes went blank. Her breathing became slow and regular, and all the personality went out of her face as the muscles slackened. Hunter looked away. It wasn't the first time he'd seen an esper in deep trance, but it never failed to disturb him. It was like looking at a death mask. DeChance opened her eyes, and her face took on shape and meaning again, as a glove does when a hand fills it.

"There's something there, Captain, but nothing I can get a hold on. Whatever it is, it's awake and aware and in pain. Terrible, maddening pain. I thought at first it might be dreaming; it was a lot like watching a nightmare from the outside. But the pain's too real for that."

"Be more specific," said Hunter. "Are you talking about a single creature? That's all there is in the forest?"

"I don't know. Possibly. It's unlike anything I've ever encountered." DeChance paused for a moment, and then fixed Hunter with her unsettling pale eyes. "I can't find a trace of any other life in the forest, Captain. No animals, no birds, no insects. There's a chance that what I'm picking up is the forest itself; a single living organism."

Hunter turned to the Investigator. "Is that possible?"

Krystel shrugged. "Group minds have been a popular theory for years, but no one's ever found one."

"If this is a group mind, could it be dangerous?" said Hunter impatiently.

Krystel smiled. "Anything alien is dangerous, Captain."

And that puts the decision back in my hands, thought Hunter. *Go on, go round, go back.* He looked around him again. The packed ranks of brooding trees threw back his gaze with cold indifference. Hunter hesitated, uncertain what to do for the best. He could still turn around and go back, but as yet they hadn't come across anything actually threatening. On the other hand, the esper was right; there should have been some kind of life in the forest. Instead, it was as quiet as the grave. But they were still safer in the forest than they would be out on the plain at night. Probably . . . He looked back at his people.

"Investigator, you and I will take the point. DeChance, you and Williams stay close behind us, but don't crowd us. Yell out if you sense anything threatening. Corbie, Lindholm, you bring up the rear. Guns at the ready, people; if in doubt, shoot first and ask questions later. I don't want anyone or anything getting closer to us than ten feet. Got it?"

Everyone nodded. Williams raised a tentative hand.

"Yes, Doctor. What is it?"

"Shouldn't we activate our force shields, Captain? Just in case?"

"It's up to you, but bear in mind they'll drain their energy crystals dry after only a few hours' continuous use. You might prefer to save your shield for when you really need it."

Williams flushed, and nodded quickly. Hunter moved off into the gloom, and the others followed.

The smell grew worse. A damp, acrid smell of drifting smoke and crushed leaves. The ground underfoot became broken and uneven, rising here and there in crooked ridges as tree roots rose up against the surface. The gloom pressed close about the narrow trail. The Squad's footsteps sounded loud and clear on the quiet, but the tightly packed trees soaked up the echoes almost before they started.

Corbie clutched his gun so tightly his fingers ached. He was scared again, and had to fight to keep it out of his face. He had enough pride left for that at least. He and Lindholm were supposed to be the Squad's fighters, their defenders and protectors. The others depended on them. Corbie almost managed a smile at that, but it wasn't much of a smile. It had been a long time since he'd been able to protect anyone, including himself. There had been a time when drink had given him the courage he needed to get through each day, but for some months now even that hadn't been enough. Everyday problems and difficulties had become increasingly difficult to deal with. Anything beyond the routine had become suspect and even terrifying. He was tense all the time, and his muscles ached. He didn't sleep much, and when he did, he had bad dreams.

After the war against the Ghost Warriors, something had broken inside him and never mended. It was getting harder and harder for him to hide the fact, but for the moment at least he still had his pride, and he wouldn't give that up. It was all he had left. Besides, he couldn't show his shame in front of Lindholm. The man was a legend in the Arenas; took on all comers for three years and never once looked like losing. There were rumours he'd killed a Wampyr with his bare hands in a private match. Corbie smiled sourly. Maybe that was why he stayed so close to Lindholm, hoping some of the courage would rub off.

He didn't like the forest. The shadows were too dark, and the quiet had the texture of something only rarely disturbed. Corbie glared about him and licked his dry lips compulsively. Something felt wrong. He couldn't see or hear anything specific that he could blame for his unease, but his instincts were yelling so loudly his stomach was cramping in sympathy. At first he'd dismissed it as just more of his nerves at work, but he was still too much the professional to believe that for long. The esper was right. The Squad was being watched. A shadow moved at the corner of his vision, and Corbie had to use all his self-control to stop his head from turning to follow it. He stared straight ahead, but kept a careful watch. The movement came again.

"Captain," he said quietly. "Movement. Four o'clock."

Hunter looked casually in that direction, and then away again. "I don't see anything, Corbie."

"I did. Twice. I think it's moving along with us."

"Damn." Hunter stopped and lifted his hand. The others came to a halt. "All right, people, form a circle. Stay close, but leave yourselves enough room to use your swords. Don't use your guns unless you have to. Remember; a lot can happen in the two minutes it takes your disrupter to recharge between shots."

The Squad started to move, and the forest fell apart. A tree directly before them slumped forward like a melting candle. Leaves dripped from its branches and splashed on the ground. The gnarled trunk lost its definition and collapsed into a pool of frothing liquid that spilled sluggishly across the trail. There was a swift rasp of steel on leather as the Squad drew their swords. DeChance cried out in disgust as something soft and clinging fell onto her shoulders from above. It only took her a few seconds to realise it was just a fallen branch, and she'd just started to relax when it whipped around her throat and tightened. She clawed at it with her free hand and the branch collapsed under the pressure of her hold. It oozed between her fingers as she pulled it free and threw it away.

"Back to back!" yelled Lindholm. "Everyone back to back. And watch your neighbours as well as yourself!"

All around them the forest was melting and deforming. Shapes could not hold, and tree trunks stretched and oozed into each other. Leaves fell like rain, lying on the ground in heaps, curling and uncurling like dying moths. Branches enlongated like boiling taffy, flailing at the Squad from all sides with blind ferocity. They defended themselves with their swords, the cold steel slicing through the waving branches with hardly any effort. Claws and barbed spikes erupted suddenly from the branches, and fanged mouths yawned in the ground. Unblinking eyes stared from bubbling tree trunks. They weren't human eyes.

Corbie raised his gun and fired at the nearest tree. It exploded, sending hundreds of writhing particles flying through the forest, but even as they landed they were still pulsing, still moving, still alive. The ground began to shake underfoot. Deep in the forest, something howled wordlessly.

"Head back down the trail!" yelled Hunter. "Force shields on! Make for the boundary!"

The Squad's hands went to their bracelets, and force shields blinked into existence on their arms. The glowing oblongs of pure energy shimmered brightly in the gloom, proof against any weapon known to man. The Squad moved quickly back down the trail. Barbed roots thrust up out of the earth and stabbed at them. A tree spotted with dark, cancerous growths leaned out over the trail. Hunter raised his gun, and the tree suddenly lost all shape and form and surged towards him like a wave of dark, boiling water. He raised his shield before him, and his arm shook as the full weight of the melting tree slammed against the glowing shield and fell past its edges in bubbling streams. Corbie and Lindholm moved quickly in beside him and took some of the weight on their shields.

All around the Squad the forest was collapsing and falling apart, yet still somehow clinging to awful forms of life. The Squad edged back down the trail, a few feet at a time, force shields spitting and crackling, edge to edge, as they formed a defensive barrier round the group. The forest had become unrecognisable. Vague shapes stirred in the frothing carpet that boiled around the Squad, fountaining up into blurred forms with teeth and claws and staring eyes. The remaining trees were slumping against each other, losing definition and meaning as they mixed and merged. The living rain continued, and the shadows became subtly darker.

Hunter's breathing had become painfully quick and hurried, and he had to fight for air. All his instincts were screaming at him to cut and run for the boundary, but he couldn't do that. Panic gnawed at his courage, but he wouldn't give the forest the satisfaction of seeing him run. He had led his people into the trap, and he would lead them safely out again. Somehow he kept the fear out of his face, and if his hands trembled he wasn't alone in that. He fired his disrupter ahead of him, blowing away a mass of twitching branches that sought to block the trail. It helped to at last have something solid and real to face, so he could bury his panic in the rush of action. He glanced at Corbie and Lindholm beside him. Lindholm was smiling absently as his blade flashed out to cut through a reaching black tentacle. Corbie's sword work was slower and less sure, but he fought with a furious, dogged tenacity that kept the forest at bay. Hunter looked away, disgusted at the panic that still tore at him, blind and stupid and almost overwhelming.

If there's any hope for this Squad's survival, he thought bitterly, *it lies with those marines, not with me. They're fighting men . . . and I'm not. Not any longer.*

It seemed to take forever to reach the edge of the forest, but suddenly the gloom gave way to sharp, brilliant light, and the air was clean and fresh again. The Squad staggered away from the boundary, weak with shock and relief but still somehow holding formation and keeping their guns trained on the forest. Branches like long gnarled fingers stretched out after the Squad with slow, sinuous movements, but seemed unable to pass far beyond the forest's boundary. Hunter slowly lowered his gun and turned off his force shield, and one by one the others did the same.

"Looks like you were right, esper," said the Investigator calmly. "The forest is alive and aware."

"Smells more like it's been dead for months," said Corbie. He scrubbed determinedly at the black stains that fouled his uniform, quietly pleased that his voice sounded calm and steady.

The Squad cleaned themselves up as best they could, brushing away the marks the forest had left on them. A thick, viscous slime clung to their clothes and skin. It seemed to pulse slowly with a life of its own and had an unpleasant fleshy feel. The Squad took turns scraping it off each other's backs and shoulders.

"No wonder there weren't any birds or animals in the forest," said Hunter finally. "The forest must have eaten them all. That damn stuff's got the perfect camouflage. You don't realise you're in any danger till you're right in the middle of it." He turned to DeChance. "What can you sense now, esper?"

DeChance frowned. "Nothing clear. Hunger. Rage. Pain. And other things I don't recognise. If they're emotions, they've no human equivalent."

"What are we going to do now, Captain?" Williams' voice was polite but pointed. "We can't go through the forest, but going round it will add miles to our route."

"Then we'll just have to walk a little further," said Hunter. "The exercise will do us good."

He kept his voice carefully easy and relaxed. It now seemed certain they'd have to spend the night out in the open, the one thing he'd wanted to avoid, but there was no point in worrying his people unnecessarily. They should be safe enough, provided they took reasonable precautions.

Krystel looked thoughtfully at the forest. The trees at the boundary had resumed their normal shape, but beyond them there was only a seething darkness. "I think we were lucky in there, Captain. The forest could have killed us all if it had reacted to us quicker."

"It was asleep," said Megan DeChance. "It had been asleep for a long time. We woke it up."

Hunter looked sharply at the esper. Her voice was slow and slurred, and her pale eyes were vague and lost. She stood facing the forest, but her gaze seemed fixed on something far beyond. The Squad looked at each other uncertainly. Lindholm took her by the arm and shook her gently, but she didn't respond. Hunter gestured for the marine to leave her be, and stepped in close beside her.

"It's been asleep a long time," said the esper. "Dreaming. Stirring occasionally as the world turned. It's all been asleep. . . ."

"What has, Megan?" asked Hunter softly.

"Everything." Her eyes suddenly cleared, and she shook her head dazedly. "Captain, I . . . don't know what I was picking up there. I was tapping into something immense, but it was so strange, so . . ."

"Alien," said Investigator Krystel.

"Yes," said DeChance, almost reluctantly. "I'm sorry I can't be more specific, Captain. I've never felt anything like that before. I didn't begin that trance; something called to me. Something . . . horrible."

The simple loathing in her voice silenced the Squad for a while. Hunter was the first to pull himself together.

"All right," he said briskly. "Keep listening. If whatever it was tries to contact you again, let me know immediately." He looked away from the esper and scowled at the forest. If there was something out there watching for them, it might be best to provide it with a smaller target . . . or two.

He turned his back on the forest and addressed the Squad. "We're going to split into two groups, people. The Investigator, Dr. Williams, and I will try the western route round the forest. The rest of you will follow the eastern route. Take your time, keep it quiet, and keep your heads down. Two small parties should be harder to spot than one big one, but only as long as we're careful not to draw attention to ourselves. The two routes looked to be pretty much equal in length on the computer map, but the terrain is different; that could cause difficulties. Whichever group gets to the city first is to wait at the boundary until the other team joins up with them. That's an order. DeChance, you're in charge of your group. Remember, everyone, the purpose of this little trip is to gather information, not to take needless risks. All right, that's it. Let's go, people."

The two marines nodded briefly, and then set off towards the east with Megan DeChance. Hunter watched the esper go, and frowned thoughtfully. He had no doubts about Lindholm and Corbie; they could look after themselves. But the esper . . . that last trance of hers worried him. She'd looked . . . different, out of control somehow, as though the contact had briefly overwhelmed her. He sighed quietly. The trouble with espers was that they were so damned spooky even under normal conditions, you couldn't be sure if there was anything wrong with them or not.

It was asleep. We woke it up.

Woke what up? Hunter scowled. There were always more questions, and never enough answers to go round. Still, the odds were the city would change all that. One way or another. Hunter nodded abruptly to the doctor and the Investigator, and set off towards the west, giving the forest boundary a more than comfortable margin. Williams and Krystel followed silently after him.

Behind them, the forest moved through shape after shape, searching through memories of times long gone for one form it could hold to.

They walked in silence for the best part of an hour. The forest gradually began to settle back into stillness, and the trees at the forest's boundary became firm and solid. Dirty yellow leaves hung from steady iron-black branches, and the gnarled boles were thick and sturdy. But further within, the darkness still stirred and writhed. Indistinct forms came and went, and the few shapes Hunter could make out were strangely disturbing, as though they hovered on the edge of meaning without ever achieving it. His hand itched for his disrupter. The forest offended him. He wanted to burn it to the ground, cleanse it with fire, punish it for pretending to be something it wasn't. In an alien world, where nothing looks or feels right, there's a constant temptation to see the familiar in things that bear only a slight resemblance to the original memory. The forest had looked reassuringly normal, almost comforting. Hunter had badly wanted to find at least one place on his new world where he could feel safe and at ease. Now that had been denied him. The forest had betrayed him by being alien.

Investigator Krystel studied her two companions dispassionately as they walked along together. The Captain was going to be a problem. He wasn't being decisive enough. From her own experience in the field she knew that staying alive on an alien world depended on quick thinking and quicker reflexes. If the Captain had listened to the esper's warnings, the forest wouldn't have caught them unaware. The Captain was too trusting. Krystel smiled slightly. There was only one rule to follow in studying the alien: be prepared to shoot first.

She had her orders. In the event that Hunter proved unsatisfactory as team leader, she was to replace him. By force, if necessary. It shouldn't be too difficult. The doctor wouldn't oppose her; he was weak, and easily swayed. The marines would follow orders, no matter who they came from, providing they were given confidently enough. And the esper would do as she was told. Espers knew their place. But when all was said and done, Krystel had no wish to be team leader. She didn't care for the work or the responsibility of giving orders. She worked best when others set the goals and restrictions for her. She knew where she was then. Her role as Investigator left her free to concentrate on the things that really interested her. Like killing aliens. So she'd give Hunter all the rope he needed. And only hang him with it if it proved necessary.

The alien city troubled her. Technically, she should have insisted on contacting the Empire the moment they discovered the city's existence, but she didn't want to do that, just yet. Firstly, she'd look a fool if it turned out to be nothing more than a deserted ruin. They'd accuse her of panicking. And secondly, if she reported the city, the Empire would take it away from her. They wouldn't trust her to do the job properly; not after Grendel. The Fleet would send their own team in, and they'd get all the glory. Krystel wanted this city for herself. She'd use it to prove to the Empire that they'd been wrong about her. She was still an Investigator.

She tapped into the pinnace's computers, and ran the records on the city. The strange towers and monoliths lay superimposed on the scene before her, like pale, disturbing ghosts. The patterns and buildings matched nothing she'd seen anywhere else, which was something of a relief. The Empire's main fear had always been that someday it would run into an alien counterpart. So far, interstellar war was nothing more than a computer fantasy, and everyone fervently hoped it would stay that way. After the discoveries on Grendel, the computer predictions had become increasingly gloomy. Whatever had created the living killing machines on Grendel was quite possibly even more deadly and implacable than the Empire itself.

Aliens. As yet there had been no sightings of who or whatever built the city, but still Krystel felt a familiar tingle of excitement running through her at the thought of encountering a new alien species. There was something about the use of sword and gun that brought her truly alive. All Investigators knew a single truth, and based their lives around it. Mankind has always achieved its best in the pursuit of violence. Investigators were the end result of society's search for the perfect killer; the most deadly weapon humanity could forge.

And like all weapons, they needed constant tempering in the heat of battle to maintain their strength and cutting edge.

Williams tried to keep his eyes away from the melting forest, and concentrated on the alien city. There was money to be made there; he could feel it. But the Captain was going to be a problem. Dictatorial, overbearing, and too straitlaced for his own good, that one. If there were any profits to be made from this world, Williams had a strong feeling it would be in spite of, rather than because of, Captain Hunter. Still . . . Williams smiled slightly. It was a dangerous world. It was always possible the Captain would have an accident. A very regrettable, but thoroughly fatal accident.

The forest moved slowly past them as they made their way round its perimeter. Hunter kept a careful eye on the frozen boundary, but the forest made no threatening moves. He began to breathe more easily. Perhaps the forest was going back to sleep again.

The bright sun was high in the morning sky when they came across the water hole. It was roughly circular, some ten feet across, and maybe a dozen yards away from the forest boundary. Hunter brought the group to a halt, and stood a cautious distance away from the water hole while he studied it. The water lay a foot or so beneath the level of the surrounding ground, which was dry and rock-hard, just like everywhere else. The water was a dark crimson colour, and when Hunter leaned forward he caught a whiff of a faint, sharp smell he couldn't identify. The sides of the hole were scalloped in a series of regular markings, and looked as though they'd be unpleasantly slick and smooth to the touch.

'We'd better mark the hole's position," said Hunter finally. "We're going to need a supply of fresh water soon."

"Assuming that stuff's drinkable," said Krystel. "We only have a limited supply of purification tablets."

"Yeah." Hunter frowned. "I should have brought some dowsing equipment, so I could run tests on freely-occurring water. It's one of the things we're going to have to sort out fairly quickly. Damn."

"Don't care much for the colour," said Krystel. "Or the smell."

"Perhaps I can help," said Williams. He moved forward slowly, keeping a watchful eye on the water hole, and then knelt down beside it.

Hunter drew his gun and trained it on the well. "That's close enough, Doctor. What did you have in mind?"

Williams held up his left hand, and retractable sharp-edged sensor spikes emerged from under his fingernails. "I have a number of options built in, Captain. You never know when they'll come in handy. Now, with your permission . . ."

Hunter looked around. The forest was still and quiet, and the open plain was bare and empty for as far as he could see. "All right, Doctor; go ahead. But be very careful. There's no telling how far down that water goes, or what else might be in it apart from water."

"Understood, Captain." Williams leaned forward, and lowered his fingertips into the water. The extruded sensors glowed faintly; five shimmering sparks in the crimson water. Bright metallic lettering appeared before his eyes, detailing the water's ingredients.

"Well?" said Hunter. "Is it drinkable?"

"I'm afraid not, Captain. This stuff's more like soup than water. Most unusual makeup. I'm reading metallic salts, a fairly high acid level, and what appears to be some kind of enzymes."

Krystel frowned. "That isn't a naturally occurring mixture, Captain. It sounds more . . . organic."

"Yeah," said Hunter. "I think you'd better get away from there, Doctor."

Williams drew his hand back out of the water, and the dweller below struck quickly while its prey was still within range. A dark blue tentacle shot up out of the water and slapped around Williams' wrist. He screamed with pain as the hold tightened viciously, and had to brace his legs against the side of the well to keep from being drawn in. The tentacle snapped taut.

Hunter fired instinctively with his disrupter, and severed the tentacle. Williams fell backwards, and scrambled away from the water hole without bothering to get up. The severed tentacle thrashed back and forth in the water. Pale purple blood flew on the air. Hunter stepped back to avoid it, and three more tentacles erupted out of the churning water, attracted by the movement. They whipped around Hunter, pinning his arms to his sides, and then snapped taut. Hunter crashed to the ground, and fought desperately against the tentacles' pull. Their hold tightened, and hundreds of miniscule barbs grated against his steelmesh tunic.

Krystel drew her sword and cut at the nearest tentacle. The sharp edge barely penetrated the leathery flesh, and she sawed at the tentacle to try and weaken it. The Captain was dragged steadily closer to the well's edge, despite all his struggles. Krystel glared at Williams, who was sitting nursing his bruised wrist.

"Grab him, dammit; I can't do it all myself!"

For a moment, Williams was tempted to tell her to go to hell. He wasn't about to risk his life for the Captain's. One look at Krystel changed that. He wasn't stupid enough to get an Investigator mad at him. He moved quickly forward and grabbed Hunter's legs. The extra weight slowed the tentacles down, but Hunter was still being drawn closer to the water's edge. Krystel sheathed her sword, drew her gun, and fired into the water. The tentacles writhed, slamming Hunter and Williams against the ground, but didn't release their hold. Krystel swore unemotionally, and put away her gun. She unclipped a concussion grenade from her bandolier, primed it, and tossed the grenade into the middle of the well. It quickly disappeared, and for a long moment nothing happened. The tentacles snapped taut again, and Hunter dug his heels in against the broken ground. Williams clung to the Captain's legs and swore breathlessly.

Water fountained up out of the well as the grenade exploded down below. The tentacles bucked and heaved, casting Hunter and Williams away. The water boiled and frothed, and chunks of partially broiled flesh bobbed to the surface. The tentacles whipped back into the water and disappeared. The surface of the water gradually grew still, and a long, peaceful silence fell over the water hole.

"Is there any life form on this planet that isn't treacherous and disgusting?" said Hunter, sitting up slowly and carefully.

"Early days yet, Captain," said Krystel, lighting a new cigar. "The rest could be downright devious."

Williams got unsteadily to his feet. "I think we should all return to the pinnace. The Captain and I could both be suffering from internal injuries."

"Don't make such a drama out of it," said Hunter. He rose to his feet and made a token attempt at brushing the dirt from his uniform. "We're just bruised and battered, that's all. Now let's get moving again. The sooner we put some distance between us and whatever it is that's living at the bottom of that well, the better I'll like it. And in future, if we come across any other water holes, I think we'll drop a grenade down it first, and check the quality of the water afterwards."

He turned his back on the water hole and walked away. Krystel and Williams exchanged a glance, and moved off after him.

Corbie and Lindholm strolled unhurriedly after Megan DeChance as they left the melting forest behind them and headed out over the broken plain. The esper was some way ahead of the two marines, and the gap was slowly widening. DeChance glanced back over her shoulder, her face set and grim. She was tempted to order them to walk faster, but she had a strong feeling they'd just ignore her. Technically, she was of a superior rank, and the Captain had specifically put her in charge of the group. But none of that mattered a damn; Megan DeChance was an esper.

Espers had a contradictory status in the Empire. On the one hand, their powers made them invaluable servants, much sought after and prized. But those same powers made them officially sanctioned pariahs, feared and detested by those in authority. Espers were conditioned from their earliest childhood to know their place; to be meek and obedient and cooperative, and never, ever, to challenge authority. Those who had trouble learning these lessons found them brutally enforced. All espers carried some scars, physical and mental. They were second-class citizens, tolerated only because they were needed. Every esper dreamed of escape, but there was only one sanctuary from the Empire, and that was the rebel planet Mistworld. Getting there was a long and dangerous journey, and only a few ever made it. Megan DeChance hadn't even got close. Which was possibly why she'd been allowed to join a Hell Squad instead of the body banks.

Corbie didn't give a damn about espers, one way or the other. He didn't trust them, but then Corbie didn't trust anyone, including himself. If you don't trust anyone, they can't let you down. As for the esper's authority, if she didn't push her luck, he wouldn't either. He was in no hurry to get to the alien city. Let the Captain and his team get there first. They had the Investigator.

He looked disinterestedly around him as he strolled along. The plain rose steadily before him, and then fell away again. Banks of pale red clouds sailed majestically overhead, clashing gaudily with the green sky. The ground was hard and unyielding under his feet, and covered with endless cracks. Corbie supposed he must have seen a more desolate landscape somewhere before, but he was damned if he could think when.

They'd just crossed the high ridge when a low, rumbling sound suddenly broke the silence and the ground shifted slightly underfoot. Corbie and Lindholm stopped dead in their tracks and looked quickly around them, but the wide-open plain below was bare and deserted. Megan DeChance hurried back to join them, and the two marines moved automatically to protect her with their bodies in case of attack. The ground slowly grew still, but the rumbling sound continued, growing louder and more ominous. Corbie dropped his hand to his gun and glanced at Lindholm.

"What the hell is it, Sven?"

Lindholm shrugged, his face impassive. "Could be building to an earthquake. You're bound to have some earth disturbance with so much volcanic activity going on. It would explain why the ground's so broken up."

"It's not an earthquake," said DeChance slowly. "I've seen this kind of terrain before. This is geyser country. Keep watching. They should start spouting any time now."

Almost as she spoke, on the plain below a jet of boiling white water burst up out of one of the cracks in the ground and fountained high up into the sky. The water roared like a wounded animal, a deep grating sound that resonated in rhythm with the shaking ground. The fountain seemed to hesitate at the top of its reach before falling reluctantly back to the parched earth. The cracked ground drank up the water thirstily. One after another, a dozen and more geysers burst up out of the ground, mud and boiling water flying up into the green sky at heart-stopping speed. The roar of the geysers became deafening. Corbie turned to ask DeChance a question, but the noise of the eruptions drowned him out no matter how loudly he shouted. In the end, he gave up, and just watched the towering fountains as they soared into the air. Finally, one by one, the geysers fell away and disappeared as the underground pressure that fed them collapsed. A light mist of water droplets added a haze to the air. The ground rumbled quietly to itself for a while, and then fell still.

"Impressive," said Lindholm.

"Yeah," said Corbie. "It's a good thing we stopped where we did. If we'd been walking through that area when the geysers started spouting . . ." He shook his head quickly, and then looked at DeChance. "You're in charge, ma'am. What do we do now? Turn around and go back?"

"It might come to that," said DeChance. "But I don't think so. Geysers usually spout at regular intervals. As long as we time it right, we should be able to walk right through the area while they're quiet, and be safely beyond them before they spout again."

Lindholm nodded slowly. "We'd have to time it exactly right. And even then, we couldn't be sure. Those geysers were quiet until we approached. It's possible our presence set them off. If that's so, the timing of the eruptions might change as we move."

"Unlikely," said DeChance. "We just couldn't see them until we topped this ridge. This area should be within range of the pinnace's sensors. All we have to do is wait for the geysers to blow again, then patch into the ship's computers, and they'll give us the exact times."

Corbie scowled unhappily, but held his peace. He'd have leaped at any excuse that would let him turn back, but he couldn't give up while the others were still willing to go on. No matter how scared he was. The three of them stood together patiently, waiting for the geysers, and some twenty minutes later they blew again, filling the air with steam and mud and boiling water. After they died away, the ground shook and rumbled under their feet for a disturbingly long time before growing still. DeChance patched into the pinnace's computers through her comm implant, and studied the glowing figures as they appeared before her eyes.

"All right," she said finally. "The interval is twenty-two minutes. Then there's only a few seconds before the rest start to go off. The geysers seem to be limited to one small area, and we can cross that in ten minutes easily. So, as long as we keep moving, we shouldn't have any problems at all."

"Oh sure," said Corbie. "Just a comfortable little stroll, right?"

"Right," said DeChance.

"And what if we've got it wrong, and the geysers don't blow off at regular intervals, but just when they damn well feel like it?"

Lindholm smiled. "You can always say *I told you so.*"

Corbie gave Lindholm a hard look. DeChance looked away to hide a smile.

They waited in silence for the geysers to spout again. Corbie chewed the insides of his cheeks, and clenched and unclenched his hands. He hated having to wait. It gave the fear longer to build; more of a chance to get a hold on him. He watched Lindholm out of the corner of his eye, but Sven seemed as calm and as unmoved as ever. There were times, when his nerves were really bad, that Corbie thought it might help if he could just talk to someone about his fear. But Corbie was a loner, and always had been. He'd never found it easy to make friends; never wanted or needed them, really. Sven was the nearest thing he had to a close friend, but Corbie couldn't talk to him. What could a man like Lindholm, a career marine and ex-gladiator, really understand about fear?

And then the ground shook and the geysers blew, and there was no time for thinking anymore. DeChance waited until the last geyser had stopped, and then ran down onto the plain. Lindholm started after her, and then stopped as he realised Corbie hadn't moved.

"Come on, Russ; we're short on time, remember?"

Corbie tried to move, and couldn't. The geysers were out there, waiting for him, waiting for the chance to kill him. He knew that wasn't true. He knew he had plenty of time. But he still couldn't move, still couldn't run forward into danger. DeChance was already well ahead of him, running freely and easily, as though she didn't have a care in the world. Lindholm was looking at him, puzzled and impatient, but a glimmer of understanding was starting to form in his eyes. Corbie looked quickly away, anger and shame burning within him. And then DeChance screamed, and everything changed.

Corbie looked round just in time to see the cracked and broken earth collapse beneath the esper. The ground rumbled and shifted under Corbie's feet, and for one horrible moment he thought there was going to be an earthquake after all. The moment passed, and the geysers remained silent, but the esper had disappeared into a wide crevasse that looked to be a dozen yards long and still spreading. Corbie ran forward, with Lindholm close behind him.

"How much time do we have, Sven?"

"Plenty," said Lindholm. "As long as we don't run into any complications."

"Like an esper with a broken leg?"

"Right. Think positively, Russ."

They soon reached the gaping crevasse, and stopped at the edge to peer down into it. DeChance looked up at them, her face pinched and white with pain. When she spoke her voice was strained, but even.

"First the good news; I don't think I've broken anything. The bad news is, my right foot's stuck in this crack and I can't get it loose. The really bad news is that there's a geyser opening down here right next to me."

"Take it easy," said Lindholm. "We'll get you out. There's plenty of time. Right, Russ?"

"Yeah," said Corbie. "No problem. Hang on, esper, and I'll come down there with you."

He clambered awkwardly over the edge, and climbed carefully down into the crevasse. It was a good eight or nine feet deep, and underneath the cracked surface the earth was a dry, brittle honeycomb. The esper's right foot disappeared into the floor of the crevasse, swallowing up her leg almost to the knee. Corbie crouched down beside her and gently investigated the crack with his hands. The esper's boot had sunk deep into the earth honeycomb, and the broken shards were pressing against the boot like so many barbs. The harder she pulled, the harder they dug in.

Corbie swore silently. Brute force wasn't going to get her out of this, but he was damned if he could think of anything else. Time was the problem. Whatever he was going to do, he had to do it quickly. He glanced at the geyser opening next to the esper, and patched into the pinnace's computers. Glowing numerals appeared at the bottom of his vision, giving him a countdown till the geyser spouted.

4:43.

"Get out of here," said DeChance.

"Shut up," said Corbie. "I'm thinking."

"You can't stay," said DeChance evenly. "I'm trapped here, and there isn't enough time for you to get me out and get clear of the other geysers. If you stay, we'll all die."

"She has a point, Russ," said Lindholm. "There's nothing we can do for her. Except give her an easy death, instead of a hard one."

Corbie looked up angrily. Lindholm had his disrupter out and aimed at DeChance. Corbie drew his own gun. "That's

not the way we do things in the marines, Sven, and you
know it. Now throw your gun down here."

Lindholm looked at him thoughtfully.

"Dammit, Sven, throw the gun down here! I've got an
idea!"

3:24.

Lindholm threw the gun down to Corbie, who caught it
deftly with his left hand and tucked it into his belt. His
face was beaded with sweat, not just from the heat of the
geyser's opening.

"All right, Sven; get going. We'll catch you up."

"Not a chance," said Lindholm. "I want to see what
you're going to do."

Corbie flashed him a quick grin, and then aimed his
disrupter at the earth honeycomb a few inches away from
the esper's trapped foot. "Hold very still, DeChance. Don't
even breathe heavy."

He fired the disrupter into the ground. The bright energy
beam drilled cleanly through the earth, throwing broken
shards into the air. DeChance tugged at her trapped foot.
It moved a little, but remained stuck. Corbie tossed his gun
up to Lindholm, drew the second gun, and took aim at the
earth on the other side of the trapped foot. He fired again,
and the honeycomb crumbled and fell away. DeChance
pulled her foot free.

"Nice shooting, Corbie. Now let's get the hell out of
here."

"Good idea."

He holstered his gun and helped her up out of the crevasse.

2:35.

Corbie scrambled out after her, and the three of them
ran through the field of about-to-erupt geysers. DeChance
was favouring her right foot, but still running strongly.
The broken ground rumbled under their feet. A few wisps
of steam rose from geyser openings. The earth collapsed
suddenly under Lindholm's feet, but he hurdled the opening
crevasse and kept running.

1:07.

Corbie's breath was burning in his lungs, but he forced himself to run faster. Lindholm and DeChance pounded along beside him. The ground shook and rumbled under their feet, and Corbie could almost feel the pressure building down below.

:41.

Corbie glanced back over his shoulder. They'd covered a lot of distance. The esper's pace was slowing as she struggled for breath. Surely they were out of the field by now. . . .

:01.

Boiling water fountained into the air a few yards to their left. The three of them kept running, and only a few sizzling spots hit them. More geysers blew off, spouting steam and water and boiling mud, but they were all well behind the running marines and the esper.

"I should never have agreed to join the Hell Squad," said Lindholm breathlessly. "I was safer in the Arenas."

"Save your breath," panted Corbie. "You're going to need it. We're not out of the geysers yet."

"Don't you have a plan to get us out of this, Russ?"

"Shut up and keep running."

"That's a good plan."

Behind and around them, the geysers spouted hundreds of feet into the pale green skies, but the marines and the esper were already leaving them behind.

We're going to make it, thought Corbie incredulously. *We're going to bloody well make it!*

He grinned harshly as he ran. This new world was just as tough as he'd feared it would be; but just possibly he was tough enough to deal with it. Another geyser blew off, some way behind him. He tucked his chin in, and kept running.

The sky was darkening towards evening when Hunter first saw the statues. The sun was hidden behind dark clouds, and the sky's color was deepening from chartreuse to a murky emerald. Shadows crawled across the broken land as it rose steadily towards the clouds. Hunter slowed to a halt as the ground ended suddenly in a sharp-edged ridge, and he found himself looking down a steep slope at a plain some two hundred feet below. And on the plain, standing silent and alone in a semicircle in the middle of nowhere, were the statues. Three huge black columns, starkly silhouetted against the broken land. Dr. Williams and Investigator Krystel stood on either side of Hunter, looking down at the statues, and for a long time nobody said anything.

"Our first sign of civilisation," said Krystel finally. "Captain, I have to examine those statues while there's still some light."

"Now wait a minute," said Williams quickly. "If we waste time here, we won't be able to reach the city before dark."

"We wouldn't make it in any case," said Krystel. "It's still a good seven miles away, and the sun will be down in less than an hour. We might as well make camp here as anywhere. Right, Captain?"

"It looks safe enough," said Hunter. "But they could be just grotesque rock formations, shaped by the wind."

"No," said Williams flatly. "They're statues. I can see details." The other two looked at him, and Williams smiled stiffly. "I told you I had built-in extras. My eyes have been adjusted. My vision's good up to almost three miles." He looked back at the statues, and his smile disappeared. "I can see the statues in great detail, Captain, and I don't like the look of them. They look . . . disturbing."

Hunter waited, but Williams had nothing more to say. The Investigator looked at Hunter impatiently, but he avoided her gaze, refusing to be hurried. Krystel was right; they had to make camp soon, and this was as good a place as any, with the high ridge to protect them from the wind. The bare ground offered little in the way of comfort or shelter, but after a hard day's walking Hunter felt he could sleep standing up in a hailstorm. He sighed once, quietly, and then led his team carefully down the steep and jagged slope to the plain below. He couldn't recall the last time he'd felt this tired. The ground had been uniformly hard and unyielding all day, slapping sullenly against his feet, so that just the act of walking was difficult and exhausting.

The statues drew steadily closer, and Hunter tried to concentrate on their growing details, but other thoughts kept intruding. He hadn't heard from the esper's group in hours. He was sure they'd have contacted him if anything had happened, but still their silence nagged at his nerves. He didn't want to have to contact them first; that might look as though he didn't have any confidence in them to handle their own problems. But he knew he wouldn't be able to get any sleep that night, no matter how tired he was, until he'd heard from them. He decided to wait until the sun had gone down, and if they still hadn't contacted him, he'd try and raise them himself.

They should be all right. The esper might not have much dirtside experience, but she was rated as a first-class telepath. Whatever else happened, nothing was going to sneak up on her. And when it came to physical threats, the two marines should be able to deal with anything stupid enough to annoy them. Their records had made impressive reading. If their luck had been a little better, and their criminal tendencies a little more subtle, they could have ended up as heroes rather than Hell Squad fodder. Still, for all their faults they were both experienced men, and had seen combat duty on more than one alien world. And while ordinarily Hunter wouldn't have trusted either of them further than he could spit into the wind, they were both bright enough to realise they were going to need the esper's help just to stay alive on Wolf IV. They'd look after her. He remembered his encounter with the dweller in the water hole, and smiled wryly. The two marines would have made short work of that. Assuming they'd have been stupid enough to get caught by it. If there was one thing their records agreed on, it was that they trusted nothing and no one; not even themselves. Which was just the attitude they'd need to survive on Wolf IV.

The huge standing stones drew nearer, and bit by bit Hunter began to see hints of shape and meaning in their design. From the distance of the ridge, he hadn't realised just how big and solid they were. All three statues were the best part of a hundred feet high, and ten feet in diameter. Each statue had to weigh countless tons, and the back of Hunter's neck prickled uneasily as he tried to figure out how and why the damn things had been brought out onto the plain, miles from anywhere. He finally came to a halt before the first of the huge statues, and Williams and the Investigator drew up beside him. The three of them stared in silence for a long time.

"Could these be a representation of the creatures that built the city?" said Williams eventually.

"If they are," said Krystel, "we'd better hope those aren't the correct dimensions."

The statues stared impassively out over the empty plain. Their details had been blurred and distorted by wind and rain, or at least Hunter hoped they had, but the three forms were still clear enough to be both fascinating and unnerving. It was hard to get a grasp on them. Each great twisting body rested on two thick elephantine legs, but there was also a nest of curling tentacles that hung from the waist to the ground. There were two sets of arms, separately jointed, that ended in clusters of smaller tentacles. Various openings spotted the body, like so many open mouths or wounds. Hunter had to fight down a sudden urge to put his hand into one of the openings, to see how deep it went. The bulky head was a nightmare mess of harsh ridges and planes, set around a gaping maw studded with thick teeth. There was no trace of any eyes, but a series of slits and shadows at the top of the head might have been something similar. The great bulk of each statue should have made the alien creatures look slow and sluggish, but instead there was an overriding impression of strength and speed and ferocity. Hunter found his hand had dropped automatically to the gun at his side. He smiled sourly, but left his hand where it was.

"Nightmares, carved in stone," muttered Williams, glancing at the other two statues. "Horrid-looking things, aren't they? How old do you suppose these carvings are, Investigator?"

"Hundreds of years," said Krystel. "Maybe more. They've obviously been exposed to the elements for some time. . . . I'll give you another question, Doctor. Why were they left out here, so far from the city? A warning, perhaps? To mark some tribal boundary?"

"Maybe this area wasn't so deserted when the statues were erected," said Hunter. "We don't know it was always like this. Personally, I'm not so sure these statues are meant to represent the creatures who built the city. It's more likely they're some kind of legendary demon, or god. I mean, look at the body. Legs *and* tentacles? It doesn't make sense. No, these statues look to me more like a combination of creatures, rather than some naturally evolved being." He looked away, and studied the sinking sun for a moment. "We're not going to make the city before night. We'll make camp here, and carry on in the morning. The ridge and the statues should provide some shelter from the elements."

"Are you sure we'll be safe out here, on our own?" said Williams, looking nervously around him. "I mean, at least the pinnace had a force screen. . . ."

"We have a portable screen, Doctor, and a good collection of proximity mines," said Krystel. "You'll be safe enough, never fear."

They moved into the wide semicircle before the three statues, and began emptying out their backpacks. Krystel collected all the proximity mines and set about planting them in a circle around the statues, establishing a basic perimeter. Hunter set up a field lantern, and soft golden light spilled out in a wide circle. The familiar gentle glow was a comfort after the harsh sunlight of Wolf IV. Everything looked the right color again. Hunter quickly assembled the portable screen, and set it for a radius of two hundred feet, just within the proximity mines. He waited impatiently while Krystel primed the mines, and then turned the screen on. A faint shimmer on the night air was the only sign the force screen was up, but Hunter could feel his muscles relaxing for the first time in hours. He turned away to help Williams unpack the field rations, while Krystel took one last look around the perimeter.

She'd done everything she could, by the book, but somehow she still felt uneasy.

Some time later, after a meal of protein cubes and distilled water, she ended up leaning against one of the statues, the cold ridged stone pressing uncomfortably into her back. She took a long slow look at the open plain, through the shimmer of the screen. Everything seemed still and quiet, but night was falling fast, and the deepening shadows gave an added sense of urgency to her uneasiness. She stubbed out the last inch of her cigar on the statue, and lit herself another. She'd considered rationing herself, on the grounds it was likely to be some time before she could hope to get a new supply of cigars, but she didn't see the point. Either way, it was going to be a hell of a long wait, so she might as well enjoy them while she had them.

She glanced across at the other two statues, and was faintly disturbed by the way the gathering shadows suggested movement in the stone faces. She tapped ash from the end of her cigar, and wished fleetingly that she was somewhere else. Anywhere else. After the mess she'd made of the Grendel mission she'd thought herself lucky to be offered a place on a Hell Squad, but she was beginning to have her doubts. As an Investigator, she'd always had the security of knowing the Imperial Fleet stood ready to back her up. Now she didn't have that anymore. She was on her own. If she screwed up again, they'd all pay for it with their lives.

Krystel smiled determinedly. She would cope. She was an Investigator.

Dr. Williams warmed his hands at the pleasant glow of heat from the field lantern. The evening was growing steadily colder, and the heating elements in his uniform could only do so much. He stretched out his left hand, and the sensor spikes slid out from under his fingernails. He slid the spikes back and forth a few times, enjoying the sensation, and then had them give him a rundown on the air around him. He didn't expect to find anything harmful, but it was a good test of the sensors' abilities. Tiny glowing numerals appeared before his eyes, via the optic nerves, giving him the exact percentages of the air's constituents. Williams ran quickly through the numbers, and then dismissed them. There were a few interesting traces, though nothing that would cause any immediate harm, and no surprises. Pretty standard air, when you got right down to it.

He retracted the sensor spikes, patched into the pinnace's computers, and had them run a systems check on his adjustments. A rush of brief sensations flowed through him, like a series of tiny sparks glowing and dying, come and gone too quickly for him to decide whether they were pleasant or not. The computers were sparking each augmentation in turn into life, just long enough for it to be checked, and then shutting it down again once it had tested out satisfactorily. The whole thing was over in a matter of seconds, and Williams smiled thinly as the computers assured him all his systems were working normally. He was sure he would have been able to tell on his own if anything was wrong, but it was as well to check while he had the chance.

He cut off the computers, and checked the readings on his implanted energy crystals. He allowed himself a small sigh of relief when they all showed a good 98 percent charge. Providing he was careful, they should last him till he could acquire some more. He tried to think what it had been like, being merely human, with no augmentations at all, and was faintly disturbed to find he couldn't remember. He frowned. It hadn't been that long ago. Perhaps it was just that he didn't want to remember. . . .

He brushed the thought briskly aside, and lay back on his bedroll. He was tired, and he'd done all the chores he intended to. If there were other things that needed doing around the camp, let the others do it. He was a scientist, not a servant. He smiled faintly, savouring the word *scientist*. He'd been the best in his field before his fall; everybody said so. Even the ones who hated him, and there were a lot of those. The Wampyr would have made him rich and famous throughout the Empire if lesser men, jealous of his success, hadn't whispered poison in the Empress's ear. . . .

Williams scowled, and then quickly composed his features in case the others were watching. One day, the Empress herself would pay for what she'd done to him. All of those who'd betrayed him would pay, and pay in blood. . . .

His hands had closed into fists, and he forced them to open again. As far as the Captain and the Investigator were concerned, he was a quiet, harmless doctor, and he wanted them to go on thinking that. There would be time for him to prove them wrong, later. There would be time for a lot of things, once the colonists finally arrived. It shouldn't be too difficult for him to bribe the supply ships to bring him the kind of high tech he needed. And with so many warm bodies available for him to experiment on, in the guise of the kindly colony doctor, who knew what triumphs he might achieve . . . ?

Captain Hunter looked distrustfully at Williams. The man was smiling again. He shook his head, and looked away. No doubt he'd find out eventually what was so damned amusing. He laid out his bedroll as far away from the doctor's as practical, and lay down on it. It felt great just to be off his aching feet at last. He stared up at the darkening night sky. The stars were coming out in ones and twos. One particularly bright light was probably one of the small moons. He started to check with the pinnace's computers, and then stopped himself. It wasn't important enough to waste valuable energy over. Hunter stretched slowly. His body was finally beginning to relax after the strain of the long walk. The ground was hard and unyielding, but he'd slept on worse in his time. He didn't expect to have any trouble about getting to sleep. Most of his body was halfway there already, and the screen and the mines would sound an alarm long before anything got close enough to the camp to be a problem.

He lay quietly, pushing back the drowsiness a little so that he could savour it. All in all, it had been an interesting first day. First the forest, then the water hole, and now the statues. Never a dull moment on Wolf IV. He smiled slightly, and rubbed gently at his bruised ribs.

He hadn't come out of it too badly, all told. He sighed, and stretched comfortably. Looking back, he was puzzled at why he'd been so scared of sleeping out in the open. Now that he was here, it wasn't that bad after all. Too much imagination, that was his trouble. He thought again about the huge standing stones looming over him, and frowned. Like most people, he'd had few actual contacts with aliens in his career, but still he couldn't help feeling there was something . . . *unnatural* about the creatures the stones depicted. They disturbed him on some very deep, very basic level. Perhaps it was the combination of features and shapes that ought not to occur together on one creature. Perhaps it was simply the overpowering size. But either way, Hunter decided that when it came time to enter the alien city the next day, he'd do it with his gun in his hand.

A yawn took him by surprise, and he closed his eyes the better to enjoy it. He quickly opened them again as he realised he'd forgotten all about the esper's group. It was well past the time he'd decided to check up on them. He activated his comm implant, and a faint hiss of static filled his ears.

"Esper DeChance, this is the Captain. Do you hear me?"

"Aye, Captain." The esper's voice was calm and clear. "We've located a sheltered area, and are settling down for the night."

"Same here. It's rather late in the evening, esper. I'd expected to hear from you earlier."

"Sorry, Captain, I just didn't have anything to report. Have you encountered any problems?"

"Nothing we couldn't handle. But if you come across any water holes, stay well clear of them. They're inhabited. Get a good night's sleep, and I'll contact you again in the morning."

"Aye, Captain. Good night."

"And DeChance . . . don't be afraid to call for help if you need it. I'd rather answer a false alarm than find I'd got there too late."

"Understood, Captain. Good night."

"Good night, esper. Pleasant dreams."

He shut off his comm unit, and tiredness rolled over him in a soft grey wave. He could see Krystel sitting with her back to one of the statues, staring out over the plain. He frowned slightly. He hadn't told her to stand guard. . . . Still, she was an Investigator, and no doubt knew her job. If she wanted to stand watch, that was up to her. Personally, he put his faith in the screen and the mines. Hunter closed his eyes, and let the day drift away.

Night sank slowly over the plain, the darkness deep and concealing, the only light the soft golden glow from the field lantern. Thin curling mists rose up around the camp, pressing close against the force screen with sullen perseverance.

Krystel sat at the base of one of the statues, at the edge of the lantern's light. The end of her cigar glowed a dull red in the gloom. She couldn't sleep, force screen or no force screen. She didn't need much sleep anyway. She was an Investigator. This wasn't the first time she'd sat guard on an alien world, but it always felt like the first. On a new world, you could never be sure what you could count on, and what would let you down. What was safe, and what was just waiting for a chance to jump you. On an unknown world, anything could turn dangerous without warning. In the end it was safest to distrust everyone and everything, and be prepared to fight for your life at a moment's notice. Not very good for the nerves, but then Investigators weren't the nervous kind.

She tensed as something stirred close at hand, and then relaxed as Captain Hunter sat down beside her.

"So, you couldn't sleep either, Investigator."

"I don't mind sitting guard, Captain. I'm used to it."

"What do you think of our new world?"

"I've seen worse."

Hunter looked at her thoughtfully. "Krystel, what was it like on Grendel?"

The Investigator took her cigar out of her mouth and blew a perfect smoke ring. She watched the smoke gradually dissipate into the air. When she finally spoke, her voice was calm and even, and only a little bitter.

"It was my first major assignment. I did a good job on Loki, and my reward was a posting to the archeological digs on Grendel. It wasn't called Grendel then, of course. We didn't know what was waiting for us.

"It should have been a simple, straightforward job, examining some ancient ruins and a few scraps of alien machinery discovered by the first wave of colonists. I should have known it was going to turn bad, the moment I set eyes on the city. The buildings on the surface were just gutted husks, but as we dug down, deeper and deeper, we came across structures so well preserved that they might have been abandoned only the day before. After a while we stopped digging; we couldn't stand the sight of what we'd found.

"The city spread out for miles beneath the surface, complete and intact. It was a nightmare of steel and flesh; a combination of breathing metal and silver-wired meat. There were rounded cylinders like gleaming, oily intestines, and pumps that beat like hearts. There were creatures that had become part of functioning machines, and complex devices with eyes and entrails. We found thinking machines that looked as though they'd been grown as much as built. It wasn't the first time I'd seen such things. The crashed alien ship on Unseeli had been . . . similar, but the city was worse. Much worse. Whoever or whatever built and then abandoned the city wasn't sane, in any way that we might understand the word.

"Under the city we found the vaults. They were huge, monumental; as clean and shining as though they'd been built yesterday. They were locked tight, with no sign to show what they held. We all had different theories as to what the vaults contained, but we all wanted to open them. We'd never seen anything like the city, and we had to know more.

"Looking back, I think we were all a little crazy by then. We'd spent too long down in the city, away from the sane everyday world above. I was in charge, so the final decision was mine. I was the Investigator, trained in the arts of understanding and destroying alien cultures. The city was vile, but so far we hadn't come across anything actually threatening. And after all, Empire troops were only a distress-call away. Despite everything, I was still cautious—we all were—but none of us really believed there was anything in the vaults that could possibly prove a threat to the might of the Empire.

"So we blasted open the vaults, and the Sleepers awoke.

"We lost twenty men in the first few minutes. Our weapons were all but useless against the devils we'd released. I was buried under rubble, and left for dead. You should have seen them, Captain—living metallic creatures that had been genetically designed with only one purpose in mind: to kill. Nightmares in flesh and blood and spiked silicon armour. They were huge and awful, but they moved so fast that half the time we could only see them as a blur. Their claws ripped through stone and metal as though it was paper. Their grinning mouths had gleaming steel teeth. They moved through the city and up out into the archeological digs, and there was nothing anyone could do to stop them.

"I finally dug my way out of the rubble, and followed the trail they'd left. There was blood everywhere, and bodies, and bits of bodies. All of it human. Up on the surface, the camp had been wrecked. No one was left alive. I hid in the ruins for three and a half days. It seemed like years. Finally I found a working comm unit in the wreckage of a shattered pinnace and contacted the ship in orbit. They came down and got me off."

Krystel raised her hand to her cigar, and then stopped and held her hand up before her. It was shaking slightly. She stared at it until it stopped.

"The colonists were all dead. Wiped out, to the last man, woman, and child. The Empire sent the best it had against the aliens. Seasoned attack troops, battle espers, even one company of adjusted men. None of them lasted long. Finally, the Fleet moved in and scorched the entire surface of the planet from orbit. Grendel is under quarantine now, guarded by half a dozen Imperial starcruisers. Just in case there are more sealed vaults and more Sleepers, hidden deep beneath the surface.

"And that's why I'm here with you, Captain. Because I missed the warning signs and let the creatures loose. And because I hadn't the sense to get myself honourably killed on Grendel. Maybe I'll do better this time."

They sat in silence a while, staring out at the darkness and the thickening mists beyond the force screen. Krystel turned and looked at Hunter for the first time. "So tell me, Captain, what was it like, out in the Rim worlds?"

Hunter tried to answer her, and his throat closed up on him. He struggled to get the words out anyway. She'd told him her story as honestly as she could, and he was damned if he'd do less for her.

"It's dark out there, on the Rim. The stars are scattered thinly across the gulf, and habitable planets are few and far between. Beyond the edge of our galaxy lies the endless night, a darkness so deep no ship has ever crossed it and returned. But the Rim planets are still part of the Empire, and have to be patrolled.

"Time seems to move differently, out there. It drags on slowly, each day like the day before, until you can't tell one day from another. The endless dark preys on your nerves, like an itch you can't scratch. You begin to feel as if you've always been out on the Rim, and always will. You can't ever relax. Ships disappear on the Rim, and no one knows why. You start to look forward to trouble breaking out, because then at least there'll be some action; something to do, something to strike back at.

"I was a good soldier. I carried out my orders, defended the Empire from her enemies, and never once questioned a command. Until they made me a Captain. You see, then I had to give the orders, and more and more I found the reasons behind those orders just weren't good enough. Sometimes they didn't even make sense. But I gave the orders, and saw them followed through, because my superiors told me to. I was a good soldier. But during the endless watches, spent staring out into the starless gulf, I began to wonder if their reasons were any better than mine, if their orders were any more sensible than mine, or if we were all just stumbling blindly in the dark.

"Giving orders began to grow more difficult. Making decisions, any decisions, took more and more of an effort. I didn't trust my superiors anymore, or the Empire, and certainly not myself. I lost all sense of security, of stability. I couldn't depend on anything anymore. Just getting through the day got harder all the time. Even small, simple decisions had to be wrestled over until I nearly drove myself crazy. I started having to check things over and over, to make sure I'd done them, even though I knew I had. Sometimes I gave the same order two or three times, and checked up on my crew to be sure it had been carried out.

"People began to notice. Some of them started to talk about me. I knew, but I did nothing about it. I didn't know whether to feel worried or relieved. And then an order came through that I couldn't ignore. A starship had gone rogue in my sector. I was to hunt it down and destroy it. It wasn't difficult to find. The rogue ship turned out to be the same class as mine, and armed to the teeth. In the heat of the battle I had to give orders quickly and efficiently, and I couldn't. I panicked, unable to decide, and my ship was blown apart. I got away in one of the lifeboats. So did some of my crew. Certainly more than enough to place the blame on me.

"But I wasn't to blame. Not really. It was the Rim. All that darkness with no stars. The Rim would drive anyone over the edge if they stayed out there long enough.

"And that's why I'm here, Investigator. I lost my sense of security and stability, so they sent me here. To Hell."

He smiled briefly, and looked at the Investigator. Her face was calm and impassive, as always, and he was glad of that. If she'd shown him anything that even looked like pity, he thought he might have hit her. But she didn't say anything, and after a while he looked away again.

"Captain," said Krystel finally, "just supposing that the city does check out as harmless, and the Empire does establish a colony here, what will you do? I mean, what will you do as a colonist? They're not going to need a starship Captain."

"I hadn't really thought about it," said Hunter. "I've got my military training. That's always useful in itself. How about you?"

Krystel chuckled dryly. "I'm an Investigator, Captain. The perfect killing machine. There'll always be work for me."

Hunter was still trying to find an answer to that when the proximity mine went off. The ground shook, and an alarm rang automatically in Hunter's ears until he shut it off. The explosion seemed to echo on and on, deafeningly loud on the night's quiet. Hunter and Krystel rose quickly to their feet and stood back to back, guns in hand, searching the camp's perimeter for signs of the force screen being breached. Williams scrambled to his feet and kicked aside his bedroll as he grabbed for his gun.

"What is it? What's happening?"

"Proximity mine," said Hunter brusquely. "Something's found our camp. Stay alert and watch where you're pointing your gun."

"Two o'clock, Captain," said Krystel softly, gesturing with her gun at that part of the perimeter. "According to the computers, the rest of the mines are still active, but nothing's close enough to trigger them. The screen's still up and holding."

Hunter strained his eyes against the mists and the darkness, but the light from the field lantern didn't reach far beyond the perimeter. The mists were still curling angrily near the blast site, but there was no trace of what might have caused the explosion. Hunter hefted his gun uneasily. "Can't see a thing, Investigator. Williams, what about those augmented eyes of yours?"

"Sorry, Captain, the mists are too thick. I'm just as blind as you."

"Terrific," said Hunter.

"Quiet," said Krystel. "Listen."

They fell silent, and Hunter was struck again by how unnaturally quiet the night was. No animal cries, no birds or insects, not even the moan of the wind. But somewhere out in the night, outside the force screen, something was moving. It sounded big and heavy, and its footsteps had a slow, dragging quality. It was heading slowly around the perimeter, counterclockwise.

Widdershins, thought Hunter crazily. *It shouldn't do that. That's unlucky.*

"It should hit the next mine any second now," said Krystel quietly. "Whatever it is, it must be tough as hell. That first mine should have ruined its day permanently."

The ground shook again as the second proximity mine exploded. The mists writhed and curled at one o'clock on the perimeter, and Hunter caught a brief glimpse of something huge and dark before the mists closed over it again. The echoes of the explosion died slowly away, and then there came a high, screeching roar from beyond the force screen. It sounded clear and sharp on the quiet, continuing long after human lungs would have been able to sustain it. If there was any emotion in the sound, Hunter was unable to put a name to it.

"Captain," said Krystel urgently, "patch into the computers. Something's come in contact with the screen."

Hunter activated his comm implant, and computer images appeared via his optic nerve, superimposed over his vision. Something was pressing hard against the screen, over and over again, trying to break through. The computers measured the varying strengths of the pressure, and provided simulations of what might be causing it. Hunter's mouth went dry. Whatever was out there was apparently some twenty feet tall, weighed roughly eight to nine tons, and probably walked on two legs. The pressure readings jumped sharply as the creature beat viciously against the force screen. The high-pitched roar sounded again on the night, shrill and piercing, and then the attack stopped as suddenly as it had begun. The creature turned away from the screen, and its slow, dragging footsteps grew gradually quieter as it disappeared back into the night.

Hunter sighed slowly, and put away his gun. "Stand down, everyone. It's gone." He shut down his comm unit, and his vision returned to normal.

"What the hell was that?" said Williams shakily.

"Just a visitor," said Krystel. "Perhaps it'll come again tomorrow."

"Captain, I strongly suggest we set a watch," said Williams. He went to holster his gun, but his hand was shaking so much he had to make three attempts before he got it right. "Whatever that was might come back again, while it's still dark."

"So what if it does?" said Krystel. "It can't get through the screen."

"On the other hand," said Hunter, "the mines didn't seem to bother it much. I think a watch is a good idea, Doctor. I'll take the first shift, you'll take the second, and the Investigator can take the last. I think we'll all sleep a little better that way."

He stared grimly at the curling mists surrounding the field lantern's small circle of light. Twenty feet tall, eight to nine tons, and two mines didn't even slow it down. He just hoped it wasn't one of the things that built the city. Because if it was, tomorrow could turn out to be a very interesting day.

Night was falling by the time Megan DeChance and the marines reached the stone monolith. They stopped some distance away and studied it carefully before going any further. They'd been watching it ever since it first appeared on the horizon. Now, seen up close, it remained as dark and enigmatic as ever. The monolith was a huge stone cube, some thirty feet to a side, with an opening in the wall before them that seemed to be a doorway. The opening was ten feet high and six feet wide. It held only darkness. The rough surface of the stone was a grey so dark it was almost black. Raised lines and ridges crawled across the stone walls like petrified ivy. The monolith had a squat, solid air of permanence, as though it had always stood there and always would. Set against the darkening sky, it looked like nothing so much as an ancient, deserted mausoleum.

"I think this will serve nicely as a campsite," said DeChance finally.

Lindholm shrugged. "Why not? I've slept in worse."

"So have I," said Corbie. "And I'm still not sleeping in that bloody tomb. Just looking at it gives me the creeps. I mean, what's it doing out here, in the middle of nowhere? We're miles from the city. No, Sven, I don't like the look of this. There could be anything inside it."

"We'll check it out thoroughly before we go in," said DeChance patiently. "If I were you, I'd be more worried about what might be lurking outside this . . . structure, once darkness falls. After what we saw in and around the forest this morning, there's no telling what forms of life come out at night."

"We've still got the portable force screen," said Corbie stubbornly.

"Yes, we have," said DeChance. "But if we set up camp out on the plain, in the open, where everything can see us, there's no telling what we might attract. I don't think there's anything on this world powerful enough to break through a force screen, but I'd rather not find out I was wrong the hard way. Now be quiet, Corbie, and let me run a mental scan on the structure."

She closed her eyes, and her face went blank. The muscles in her face twitched a few times and then were still, as all trace of personality left her features. Her breathing slowed till it was barely visible. Corbie looked at her, and then looked away, unable to repress a shudder.

"Don't worry, Russ," said Lindholm quietly. "She hasn't gone far. She'll be back soon."

"Yeah," said Corbie. "That's what worries me."

DeChance's mind roamed freely over the monolith, caressing the rough surface of the stone with her esp. It felt old, very old. Time had come and gone upon the plain, and left the monolith untouched. Inside, the structure was hollow, and completely empty. DeChance didn't know whether to feel relieved or uneasy. She frowned briefly. More and more, she found the stone monolith somehow . . . unsettling. The structure wasn't a perfect square, and the extra angles and dimensions clashed unpleasantly in her mind, as though refusing to add up to the shape she saw before her. DeChance shrugged mentally. She didn't like the feel of the monolith, but there was nothing specific she could use to justify her feelings. Particularly after her teatment of Corbie. DeChance fell back into her body, and looked at Lindholm.

"All clear. The building's quite empty."

"I'm glad to hear it," said Lindholm. "If you'd care to set up camp inside the building, Russ and I will see to the defences. The sooner we get the force screen up and working, the sooner we can all relax a little."

The three of them looked at each other for a moment, each waiting for someone else to make the first move. In the end, DeChance turned away and walked calmly over to the monolith. She almost paused at the doorway, but made herself go on. If she didn't trust her esp, she could hardly expect the marines to. Once inside, she shrugged off her backpack, took out a field lantern, and turned it on. The familiar golden glow helped to reduce the stone chamber to a more comfortable size. DeChance stepped cautiously forward, holding the lantern out before her.

The interior walls looked pretty much like the exterior; rough, bare stone covered with twisting ridges and hollows. The floor was flat and even, and only the dark shadows in the corners remained at all disturbing. DeChance walked slowly round the empty chamber. The more she saw of it, the less she understood why she'd been so worried. She even began to feel a little ashamed at letting her imagination get the better of her. And then DeChance's breath caught in her throat as the lantern light showed her a single, gleaming, milky-white sphere lying on the floor in the far left-hand corner. She stared at it for a long moment. It couldn't be there. It couldn't. Her esp would have found it during the scan.

"I thought you said there was nothing in here," said Lindholm.

The esper jumped, startled, and then flushed hotly. She'd been concentrating on the chamber so much that she'd

let her psionic defences slip. She hadn't even known the
marine was there, till he'd spoken. She quickly composed
her features again.

"There shouldn't be anything in here," she said finally,
her voice calm and even. "Whatever that is, I should have
detected its presence, at least."

"Does that mean it's dangerous?" said Lindholm.

"Possibly."

"All right, that's it," said Corbie quickly, from the doorway. "Let's get the hell out of here while we still can."

"Take it easy, Russ," said Lindholm, without looking
round.

"I thought you two were seeing to our defences?" said
DeChance.

"We talked it over," said Lindholm, "and we decided we
didn't feel right about leaving you in here on your own."

"Very gallant," said DeChance. "But I can take care of
myself."

"Of course," said Lindholm. He looked thoughtfully at
the milky sphere on the floor. "Can you pick up anything
from that, now that you're closer to it?"

DeChance frowned slightly. "I can try."

She moved slowly over to the sphere, knelt down before
it, and studied it closely from all angles, taking care not to
touch it. It was about six inches in diameter, and had a
cold, pearly sheen. DeChance reached out with her mind
and gently touched the sphere with her esp.

*The sun, burning bright and foul in the shimmering sky.
Buildings tower to every side. Something dark and awful
close behind and all around. Bones stretch and twist. Flesh
flows across twitching cheekbones. Eyes turn to liquid and
run away. Creatures leaping and hopping all around, sliding and melting into each other. The scream goes on and
on and on. . . .*

DeChance jerked her mind free from the endless flow of
images. She fell backwards, her mouth working soundlessly, and when Lindholm reached out a hand to steady her,
she struck out at him blindly. He knelt down beside her
and talked slowly and soothingly until finally the wordless

panic died away and she could think again. She drew in a long, shuddering breath, and licked her dry lips.

"What happened?" said Lindholm.

"The sphere," said DeChance hoarsely. "It's a recording of some kind. A direct recording of an alien mind."

"What did you see?" asked Corbie.

DeChance shook her head slowly. "Madness. Horror and violence . . . I don't know. I'll have to think about it. In the meantime, don't either of you try and touch it. It's too easy to get lost in there. . . ."

She got to her feet, turned her back on the sphere and the marines, and started to rummage through her backpack. Corbie and Lindholm looked at each other. Lindholm shrugged and left the chamber. Corbie hesitated, and then followed him out.

Planting the proximity mines took the marines a lot longer than they'd expected. The ground was rock-hard, and yielded only grudgingly to their digging tools. Both men were sweating by the time they'd established a perimeter, and most of the light had disappeared from the sky. The golden lantern light that fell through the monolith's doorway looked warm and inviting. The two marines went back inside, rubbing at the fresh calluses on their hands, and helped DeChance finish setting up the portable force screen generator. She activated it, and all three of them relaxed a little as some of the day's tension went out of them. They laid out their bedrolls, and pecked unenthusiastically at a late supper of protein cubes and distilled water. Finally, they lay back on their bedrolls and waited for morning to come.

None of them felt much like sleeping, but they knew they ought to at least try. Come the next day, they'd need all the strength and stamina they could muster. The Captain had sounded calm and reassuring when he contacted them just after their supper, and DeChance had done her best to sound the same. Corbie had thought seriously about breaking into the conversation to say how worried he was about the monolith and the sphere recording, but in the end he decided against it. The Captain wouldn't have understood. Maybe when they reached the city tomorrow . . . Corbie had a really bad feeling about the city.

Surprisingly enough, the esper fell asleep almost immediately. Lindholm lay on his back with his eyes closed, looking as calm and unperturbed as ever. Corbie glared at both of them. He'd never felt less sleepy in his life. He gave it a while, hoping he might drop off. Then, still wide awake, he sat up quietly and hugged his knees to his chest. He'd hoped the monolith would seem less forbidding once he'd spent some time in it, but it hadn't worked out that way. The ceiling was too high, the light from the lantern couldn't seem to penetrate the corners, and even the smallest sound echoed endlessly on the quiet. He drew his disrupter from its holster and checked the energy level. It was reassuringly high, but even so it took real strength of will before Corbie could make himself holster the gun again.

"Getting jumpy, Russ."

Corbie looked round quickly. Lindholm was sitting up on his bedroll too. Corbie smiled and shrugged. "I don't like this place, Sven," he said softly, keeping his voice low to avoid waking the esper. "Mind you, when you get right down to it I'd be hard pressed to name one thing about this stinking planet that I do like. I hate it here, Sven." He rubbed at his mouth with the back of his hand, and wasn't surprised to find his hand was shaking. "I'm dry, Sven. I need a drink. I could cope with all of this much better if I could just have one good stiff drink."

"Sorry, Russ. Don't use the stuff myself. You should have smuggled a bottle onto the pinnace."

"I did. They found it." Corbie shuddered briefly. There was a faint sheen of sweat on his face, despite the cold. "I *hate* this world, Sven. I don't want to be here. It doesn't want us here. I mean, what am I doing in a Hell Squad? I was never meant to be a colonist. I've been in the Fleet since I was sixteen; never spent more than two years running on the same planet. I liked it that way. The only reason I'm here is because it looked a better bet than spending the rest of my life rotting in a military prison. Shows you what a fool I was. This place is worse than any prison."

"Take it easy, Russ."

"That's easy for you to say. You saw that forest, Sven. And the things that came up out of the ground. I've been on more worlds than I can count, seen some pretty strange things in my time, but at least they made some kind of sense. This world is insane. Like some nightmare you can't wake up from. And tomorrow we're going into a city full of buildings just like this one. I don't think I can do that. I don't think I *can*." He rubbed at his mouth again, and looked pleadingly at Lindholm. "What am I going to do, Sven? I can't stand it on this world, but I can't get off it. I'm trapped here. I can't face going into the city tomorrow, but I couldn't stand being left on my own. What am I going to *do?*"

"All right, Russ, calm down. I'm here," Lindholm cut in quickly as Corbie's voice began to rise hysterically. "Just remember you're not alone in this. We're all in the same boat. We can cope with anything, as long as we stick together. Think of all the different worlds we've seen; they all looked pretty bad at first. This is just another world, Russ; that's all. Just another world."

Corbie took a deep breath, and let it out again in a long, shuddering sigh. He shot Lindholm a grateful glance, and smiled shakily. "How do you do it, Sven? How do you stay so calm all the time? Is it something you learned in the Arenas?"

"You could say that." Lindholm stared thoughtfully out the open doorway into the darkness. "You can learn a lot in the Arenas, if you stay alive long enough. You learn not to be afraid, because that can get you killed. You learn not to make friends, because you might have to kill them the next day. You learn to take nothing for granted, not even one more day of life. And finally, you learn not to care about anything. Not the killing, not the people, not the pressure, not even your own life. When you don't care about anything, you can take any risk, face any odds. Because nothing matters anymore. Nothing at all." Lindholm looked across at Corbie. "The trouble is, Russ, even after you've left the Arenas, what you learned there goes with you. I don't feel much of anything anymore. I don't laugh, or cry, or feel scared or good. The Arenas took all that from me. There's just enough of the old me left to appreciate what I've lost. It's hard for me to get really interested in anything, Russ, because nothing really matters."

"What about me?" said Corbie slowly. "Do I matter?"

"I don't know," said Lindholm. "I remember the years we served together in the marines, but it's like remembering a dream I had long ago. Sometimes the dream is clearer than others. The rest of the time I just go through the motions. Don't depend on me, Russ. There's not enough left of me for that."

The esper moaned in her sleep, and the two marines looked across at her. DeChance was stirring uneasily.

"Nightmare," said Corbie. "Can't say I'm surprised."

The first proximity mine went off like a thunderclap, followed by two more in swift succession. The brilliant light flared against the darkness. The marines scrambled to their feet, guns in hand, and DeChance came awake with a start.

"What the hell was that?" said Corbie.

"There's something out there," said Lindholm. "Must have got too close to the mines. Turn off the lantern, Russ."

Corbie reached over quickly and turned it off. Darkness filled the monolith, as though it had never been away. Corbie tightened his grip on his gun and waited impatiently for his eyes to adjust to the gloom.

"Whatever's out there, it's not alone," he said softly. "It'd take more than one creature to set off all those mines."

"I can sense . . . something," said DeChance, frowning harshly. "It's hard to pin down. I'm picking up multiple readings, too many to count. They're moving, circling . . . they're all around us. We're surrounded."

Another mine exploded, piercing the darkness with brilliant light. Corbie caught a brief glimpse of dark uncertain shapes milling around the monolith, outside the perimeter, and then the night returned. There was a loud, dull thudding, like a giant heartbeat, as something began to pound against the force screen with horrid patience and determination. Corbie licked his dry lips repeatedly, and glared frantically into the night.

"Take it easy, Corbie," said DeChance. "The force screen will keep them out."

Bloody hell, thought Corbie. *Can everyone tell I'm a bag of nerves, even in the dark?*

"She's right," said Lindholm calmly. "The force screen was designed to stand against anything, even disrupter cannon and atomics. Nothing's going to break through the screen by brute force."

As if in answer to his words, the hammering suddenly stopped. Silence fell upon the night again, charged with hidden menace. DeChance stirred uneasily.

"They've stopped moving. They're just . . . standing there, as though they're waiting for something . . . Wait a minute—there's something else, something close. . . ."

The floor bucked suddenly under their feet, and split open with a deafening roar of rending stone. Cracks darted here and there across the broken floor as DeChance and the two marines fought to keep their balance.

"They're tunnelling up through the earth!" yelled the esper. "They're coming for us!"

"Somebody find the lantern!" roared Lindholm.

"Stuff that," said Corbie. He got down on both knees, riding the bucking floor, and thrust his disrupter into the nearest crack. He pressed the stud, and a blast of searing energy shot down into the earth. Far below, something screamed shrilly and then fell silent. Lindholm and DeChance fired their guns into the cracks, and the floor heaved once and then was still. For a long time there was only the darkness and the silence, and then DeChance stirred slowly.

"They're leaving," she said quietly. "They're all leaving."

Lindholm found the field lantern and turned it on again. The pale golden glow was a comfort after the panic-ridden dark. The floor was a mess of cracks and broken stone.

The walls and ceiling weren't much better. Corbie and Lindholm looked at each other and grinned.

"Nice shooting, Russ."

"Yeah, well," said Corbie. "You know how it is. Some things you never forget, no matter what."

CHAPTER THREE

The City

CAPTAIN Hunter and his team reached the outskirts of the alien city by mid-morning. The brilliant silver sun was high in the chartreuse sky, and the light reflecting from the city's towers was almost too bright to look at. Streamers of grey cloud sprawled across the sky like characters from an alien language, and the still air had a cold, cutting edge. Hunter hugged himself tightly, not just because of the cold. He'd been standing and staring at the city for some time, but he still couldn't get used to it. It lay spread out before him like some giant puzzle, the answer to which would make no sense to him even if he knew it.

The sheer aberrancy of the city swept over him like a numbingly cold tide. The huge buildings were jagged and asymmetrical, with sharp edges and distorted, scalloped roofs. Strange lights shone in empty windows, glaring like watching eyes. Bulky stone monoliths stood next to towers of shimmering crystal and twisted glass structures too intricate for the eye to rest easily on. There were open doorways and windows, their scale suggesting that whatever creatures used them had to be almost twice the size of Hunter and his companions. Gossamer metal threads hung between the buildings, forming slender walkways high above the ground. There was no sound on the still air, and no trace of movement anywhere in the city.

Hunter looked from one strange edifice to another, trying to find some familiar sight to rest his eyes on, but there was nothing his mind could comfortably accept. The alien architecture was subtly disturbing on some very basic level. It didn't follow any human rules of design or meaning.

The sheer size of the place gave him a bad case of the creeps. Whoever—whatever—had built this city had lived on a larger scale than humankind.

"We've been here almost an hour, Captain," said Investigator Krystel, "and there's still no sign of the other team."

"Perhaps something's happened to them," said Williams.

"They would have contacted us if they'd run into any trouble," said Hunter. "But you're right, Investigator. We can't wait here all day. I'll contact them and let them know we've arrived." He activated his comm implant, his eyes still fixed on the city before him. "Esper DeChance, this is the Captain. Report your position."

There was no reply, only an ominous silence, unbroken even by static. Hunter and Krystel looked at each other.

"Esper DeChance, this is Captain Hunter. Please report your position. Can you see the city?" He waited, but there was no response. "Lindholm, Corbie. Can you hear me? The silence dragged on. "Investigator, can you hear me through your implant?"

"Loud and clear, Captain. There's nothing wrong with our equipment."

"Then there must be something wrong at their end."

"Unless the city's interfering with the signal," said Williams.

Hunter frowned thoughtfully. "Esper DeChance, if for some reason you can hear me but cannot respond, we're about to enter the city. Somewhere near the centre is a huge copper tower. Try and join us at the tower. If you're not there by the time it gets dark, around 1900 hours, pinnace's time, we'll return to the western boundary of the city and make camp there. Captain Hunter out."

He shut down his comm implant, and looked unhappily at the city. "We've done all we can here. Let's go and take a closer look. Draw your guns, but no firing unless you've got a specific target."

He started to lead the way forward, but stopped as Krystel raised a hand.

"I should go first, Captain. I am the Investigator."

Hunter frowned slightly, and then nodded. She was within her rights. They were entering her province now. He gestured for her to proceed, and she led the way down the short slope that led to the city. Hunter followed her, and Williams brought up the rear.

The city seemed to loom even larger and more menacing as they made their way through the broad streets and alleyways that lay between the massive buildings. Towers dark as the night, studded with jagged crimson shapes, thrust up around them like imploring arms. The huge scale and overpowering size of the structures made Hunter feel like a child wandering through an adult world. The party's footsteps hardly echoed at all, the sound swallowed up almost immediately by the huge walls to either side of them. Hunter stood the silence for as long as he could, and then looked at the Investigator.

"You're the expert, Krystel. Any comments?"

"Just the obvious ones, Captain. Apart from the occasional exotic exceptions, most of these buildings are nothing more than huge slabs of stone. Judging by the battered and weathered appearance of the stone, they must have stood here for centuries. The complexity of the other structures suggests a high level of civilisation, so why did the city's occupants retain the primitive stone buildings? A reverence for the past? For their ancestors? Too early to tell, as yet. Maybe they just thought working in stone was artistic.

"Something else interesting. We've been walking for the best part of half an hour now, and we're well past the outskirts, but I still haven't seen a single sign to show this place was ever inhabited. Whatever happened here, it was over and finished a long time ago. Perhaps there was a war, or some kind of ecological disaster. Maybe they all committed suicide. It could even be something we don't have a name for. Understanding an alien culture takes time, Captain. Their minds don't work like ours."

"Perhaps we should take a look inside one of the buildings," said Williams diffidently. "There's only so much we can tell from the buildings' exteriors. There could be important clues inside. Who knows; we might even get lucky and find some kind of computer records."

"I'd prefer to keep moving," said Krystel evenly. "We haven't seen enough of this city to be sure it's deserted. I don't like the idea of being caught by surprise because we weren't thorough. Still, you're the Captain, Hunter; it's your decision."

Hunter stopped in the middle of the street, and the others stopped with him. He looked across at the nearest building, which appeared to have been carved from a single huge piece of crystal. Its jagged edges looked razor-sharp, and there was a crimson tracery in the smoky crystal that looked disturbingly like veins. The huge doorway was blocked by a single slab of dull metal and there were no windows. Hunter gnawed at the inside of his cheeks. There could be anything in there, watching and waiting. He didn't like that idea at all. If something or someone was watching them he wanted to know about it. And yet the more he looked at the huge crystal structure, the more uneasy he felt. He realised suddenly that he didn't want to get any closer to the building. It was too strange, too different. It felt . . . wrong. Insane.

Alien minds don't work like ours.

Hunter swallowed hard. He could feel the familiar panic building within him, the fear that whatever decision he made would be the wrong one. He had to make up his mind quickly, while he still could. "All right, people; we're going to take a look inside. Krystel, you go first. Williams, stay close to me and don't touch anything."

The Investigator nodded, and approached the doorway. Williams made as though to follow her, but Hunter held him back. The metal slab that served as a door could be booby-trapped. Krystel stood a few feet away from the door and studied it carefully. Eleven and a half feet high, seven feet wide. No handle, and no sign of any locking mechanism. There was no doorjamb; the metal butted cleanly against the crystal. She kicked the door lightly, twice. There was no response. She reached out cautiously and touched the dull metal with her fingertips.

It felt unpleasantly warm to the touch. Krystel pulled her hand back and sniffed at her fingers. There was a trace of odour, but nothing she could identify. All right; when in doubt, be direct.

She stepped back from the door, raised her disrupter, and pressed the stud. The energy bolt smashed the door inwards, leaving a jagged hole in the crystal. The Investigator moved forward slowly, stared into the opening, and then stepped through. After a moment, Hunter and Williams followed her.

It was fairly light inside the building, but it was a strange kind of illumination—the crystal diffused the daylight, giving it a smoky, dreamlike glow. The metal door lay in the middle of the room. It was twisted and crumpled, but otherwise intact. Hunter whistled silently. There wasn't a metal in the Empire that could stand up to a disrupter beam at point-blank range.

He looked slowly around him. The chamber was huge, easily fifty feet by fifty. Curved and twisted shapes dotted the crystal floor. The shapes were detailed, but essentially meaningless. They could have been furniture or statuary, or even some form of high tech for all he knew. Without a context to put them in, they could be anything. Long curving lines had been etched into the crystal walls, stretching from floor to ceiling. They served no apparent purpose.

"If there was anyone here, the noise would have brought them running by now," said Williams. He looked around him uneasily. "Maybe they all left for a reason. A good reason."

Krystel slowly approached the open doorway on the far side of the room, and Hunter and Williams followed her. If there had ever been a door to fill the gap, it was long gone. She led the way through, and they found themselves at the base of a tower. Hunter looked up the gleaming crystal shaft, and his breath caught in his throat. The tower stretched away above him for hundreds of feet, until its top was lost in the hazy light that shone through the crystal walls. *It's an optical illusion*, thought Hunter wonderingly.

It's got to be. The building isn't that tall. . . . He tore his gaze away, and studied the narrow curving ramp that spiralled up the inner wall for as far as his eyes could follow. It protruded directly from the crystal wall, with no sign of any join. It was easily six foot wide, and the surface was as smooth and unblemished as any other part of the smoky crystal.

"A ramp, instead of stairs," said Williams. "That could be significant."

"Undoubtedly," said Krystel. "But significant of what? It's too early yet to start drawing conclusions, Doctor." Her voice and face were as calm and impassive as ever, yet Hunter was sure he could detect a fire, an enthusiasm, in her that hadn't been there before. Krystel was in her element now, and it showed. She started up the ramp, her boots scuffing and sliding on the smooth crystal surface. She leaned against the inner wall to help keep her balance, and soon found the trick of keeping upright while moving on. Hunter kept to the inner wall too as he and Williams followed her, but mainly because the increasing drop worried him. There was no barrier or safety rail, and it was getting to be a long way down. The thought nagged at Hunter, and wouldn't leave him alone. What kind of being could use a ramp like this and apparently not worry about the danger of falling?

They continued up the ramp for some time, circling round and round the inside of the tower. There were plenty of doorways leading off, but Krystel kept pressing on, and the others had to follow or be left behind. Hunter's thighs started to ache, and when he looked down the shaft he could no longer see the bottom of the tower. Everywhere he looked there was nothing but scarlet-veined crystal and the diffused smoky light. He began to feel strangely disorientated, as though he'd always been climbing the ramp and always would be.

It came as something of a shock when Krystel suddenly stepped off the ramp and through an open doorway, and Hunter realised they'd reached the top of the tower. He looked quickly back to make sure Williams was still with them, and then he followed Krystel. She was standing on an open platform that looked out over the city. The platform looked distinctly fragile, but it held their weight easily enough. Again there was no safety rail, and Hunter was careful to stand a good two feet short of the edge. He looked down, and vertigo sucked at his eyes. It had to be a drop of at least three hundred feet. He would have sworn the building wasn't that tall when he entered it. The long drop didn't seem to bother the Investigator at all. She was staring out over the cityscape with something that might almost have been hunger. Hunter moved cautiously over beside her, to make room for Williams on the platform and looked out over the view.

For the first time, he could really appreciate the true size and scale of the city. It stretched away for miles in every direction, an eerie landscape of stone and metal and glass. The gossamer metal walkways looked like the spider-webs you'd expect to find on something that had been left deserted for too long. Down below, nothing moved. Everything was still and silent. But strange lights still shone in some of the windows, like so many watchful eyes, and there was a strange, palpable tension on the air.

"Well, Investigator," said Hunter finally. "This is your show. What now?"

"There's life here," said Krystel flatly. "I can feel it. The city is too clean, too untouched by time and weather to be as abandoned as it appears. So whatever lives here must be hiding from us. And in my experience, the best way to flush out something that's hiding is to set a trap, and bait it with something attractive."

"One of us," said Hunter.

"Me, to be exact," said Investigator Krystel. She smiled suddenly, and Hunter had to force himself not to look away from the hunger that burned in her eyes.

Megan DeChance and the two marines stood at the edge of the city. A row of tall, jagged towers stood like a barrier before them, dark and enigmatic in the bright midday sunlight. DeChance rubbed at her forehead. Just the sight

of the alien structures was enough to give her a headache. Her esp kept trying to make sense of the insane
shapes, and failing, unable to embrace theories of architecture and design shaped by an inhuman logic. The marines
shifted impatiently at her side. DeChance tried her comm
implant again.

"Captain Hunter, this is DeChance. Please respond."

"Still nothing?" said Corbie.

"Nothing," said DeChance.

"You could try your esp," said Lindholm.

DeChance stared at the alien city, trying to pretend she
hadn't heard him. Making telepathic contact was the obvious, logical thing to try next, and she couldn't explain even
to herself why she was so reluctant to do so. She only knew
that just the thought was enough to make her break out in
a cold sweat. She could still remember the contact she'd
made back on the pinnace, the first time she'd raised her
esp on Wolf IV. She'd found something huge and old
and powerful, something vile and awful . . . and it hadn't
been alone. Whatever it was, she was sure it lay waiting
somewhere in the city. Waiting for her to raise her esp
again, so it could find her. . . .

But she had to locate the Captain. She had to know what
was happening to the other team. And most of all she had
to face her fear, or she'd never be free of it. She could do
it. She was an Empire-trained telepath, and she could face
anything. She closed her eyes, and sent her mind up and
out, spreading across the city. At first she went tentatively,
ready to withdraw behind her shields at the first hint of
danger, but the city seemed still and silent and empty. She
spread her esp wide, but there was no trace of the Captain
or his team. Or the disturbing presence she'd sensed earlier.
She dropped back into her body, and staggered uneasily for
a moment as her headache returned, worse than ever.

"Nothing," she said bluntly. "Not a damned thing. Either
the Captain and his people haven't got here yet, or . . ."

"Or what?" said Corbie.

"I don't know." DeChance frowned thoughtfully. "I
picked up something; nothing more than an image, really,

but it might be significant. You can't see it from here, but there's a huge copper tower in the middle of the city. I think it's important in some way. Either to us, or to the city. We'll head for that. It's not much of a goal, I know, but it beats standing around here in the cold."

Corbie and Lindholm looked at each other, but said nothing. DeChance steeled herself, and led the way forward into the alien city. The marines followed her silently, guns in hand. Buildings of stone and crystal and metal loomed around them, shutting out the bright sunshine. Strange lights burned in open windows, colors slowly changing hue to no discernible pattern or purpose. The only sound was the slap of their boots on the hard, unyielding ground. The shadows were very dark and very cold.

Corbie felt the familiar prickling at the back of his neck that meant he was being watched. Military instincts might not be as officially appreciated as esp, but they could keep you alive if you listened to them. He casually studied the dark openings in the buildings around him, alert for the slightest sound or movement, but whatever was watching wasn't about to give itself away that easily. Corbie hefted the disrupter in his hand. It didn't feel as comforting as it once had. It doesn't matter how powerful a gun is, if you haven't anything to aim it at.

He didn't like the city at all. The buildings' shapes and dimensions were subtly disturbing, and the broad streets followed no pattern or design he could recognise. Each street was perfectly smooth and featureless, untouched by traffic or time. Even the air smelled wrong. The faint, sulphurous odour of the plains was gone, replaced by something oily and metallic that grated on his nerves.

"This place is dead," said Lindholm quietly. "Nothing's lived here for centuries."

"Maybe that's what we're supposed to think," said Corbie. "There's something here. I can feel it."

Lindholm shrugged. "I hope so. I'd hate to think I walked all this way for nothing."

"Are you crazy? Out on the plains we were surrounded by killer centipedes, almost eaten alive by a melting forest, not forgetting the damn geysers, and finally we were attacked in the night by something that wasn't even slowed down by a proximity mine exploding right next to it! And you want to meet whatever twisted mind thought this lot up? Come on, Sven; I hate to think what the sophisticated life forms on this planet will look like."

"You might just have something there." Lindholm glanced at one of the doors they were passing. It was easily twelve feet high and seven feet wide. "Whatever lived here was big, Russ. A race of giants. Just think about the scale."

"I'd rather not."

"Hold it." DeChance's voice cracked loudly on the quiet, and the marines stopped dead in their tracks, raising their guns reflexively.

"What is it?" said Corbie.

"I'm not sure. Let me think." She tried to raise her esp, and couldn't. The sheer alienness of the city was overpowering. "I thought I saw something moving, just on the edge of my vision. Down that way."

The marines looked where she indicated, and then looked at each other.

"It could be anything," said Corbie.

"Probably nothing," said Lindholm.

"No point in putting ourselves at risk."

"We're just a scouting party. The Captain said so."

"Even if there is something there, it could be leading us into a trap."

"Yeah. Let's go after it."

"Right."

They grinned at each other, and started off down the street. They'd given it enough time to get away, if it was just an animal. On the other hand, if it wanted them to follow it, it would still be there, waiting for them. DeChance hurried along beside them, her eyes fixed on the spot where she thought the movement had been. It turned out to be a street intersection. They stopped and looked around them. There was no sign of any living thing, but far down on the right-hand side of the street, a huge metallic door was slowly closing. DeChance and the marines moved silently towards it, guns at the ready. The door was firmly shut by the time they got there, and the featureless metal had no handle or obvious locking mechanism. Corbie blasted it open with his disrupter. The torn metal door was blown inwards by the impact. Lindholm quickly moved forward to take the point until Corbie's gun had recharged, and then one by one they stepped cautiously through the doorway.

Oval panels set into the high ceiling glowed varying shades of red, none of them very bright. The walls were a complex latticework of glistening metallic threads. Dark nodes hung in clusters here and there on the latticework, grouped in no discernible pattern. Massive, hulking alien machinery jutted from the walls and floor and ceiling. No one machine looked like any other, but they were all covered with kaleidoscopic displays of lights that hurt the eyes if stared at too long. The lights flickered on and off at irregular intervals, but there was no other sign to show how or why the machines were working. A low, almost sub-audible hum permeated the air, which had a tense, static feel.

"What the hell is this place?" said Lindholm.

"Beats me," said Corbie. "But it must be important if the machines here are still working, long after everything else has shut down. Look how clean and immaculate it is in here. The rest of the city looks like it's been deserted for centuries, but as far as these machines are concerned their operators could just have stepped outside for a moment and left things running till they got back."

"Centuries . . . ," said Lindholm. "Could they really have been running all that time, unattended?"

"I don't know. Maybe. I've got a bad feeling about this place, Sven. Let's get out of here. Now."

"Wait a minute, Russ." Lindholm looked at DeChance. "What do you think, esper? Can you tell us anything about this place?"

DeChance shook her head. "My esp's almost useless here. It's all too alien. My mind could get lost in all this.

I'm an esper, not an Investigator. Krystel might be able to make something of these machines, but they're beyond me. Could you take one of them apart and see what makes it hum?"

"Not without the right equipment," said Corbie. "And even then I'd be very reluctant to meddle with anything here. I'd hate to get one of these things doing something and then find I couldn't turn it off. Besides, I don't think I like the look of them. Sven . . ."

"Yeah, I know. You think we're being watched. I'm starting to feel that way too. It's up to you, esper. You're in charge. Do we leave, or go on?"

DeChance scowled unhappily. Without her esp to back her up, she felt blind and deaf. If they went on and there was something lying in wait for them, they could end up in real trouble. On the other hand, they couldn't afford to overlook the first sign of life they'd found. She hesitated for a long moment, torn by indecision. What would the Captain do? That thought calmed her a little. She knew what he'd do.

"I think we should check this place out," she said evenly. "Look for a door, or stairs, or something."

They made their way gingerly through the hulking alien machinery, careful not to touch anything. The constant humming of the machines hovered persistently at the edge of their hearing, like an itch they couldn't scratch. Corbie glared at the machines, and thought fleetingly that it might be fun to blast one or two of them with his disrupter, just to see what would happen. He'd never cared much for mysteries. He always liked to know what was going on and where he stood. If only so that he could set about turning things to his own advantage. He looked round quickly as Lindholm hissed to him. The big marine was standing before an open doorway in the far wall.

"Where the hell did that come from?" said Corbie quietly.

"Beats me," said Lindholm. "I'd swear it wasn't here a minute ago. Maybe we hit the opening mechanism by accident."

"Yeah. Maybe." Corbie scowled at the opening. It was dark and gloomy in the room beyond, and the pale rosy light from the machine room didn't seem to penetrate far.

Lindholm moved forward slowly, his disrupter held out before him. Corbie kept close behind him. DeChance stayed where she was. Lindholm stepped quickly through the doorway in one smooth motion, his disrupter sweeping back and forth as he looked around him for a target. A wide-open room lay spread out before him, empty and abandoned. The walls were bare and featureless, and the high ceiling was lost in shadows. Lindholm slowly lowered his gun and walked forward into the room. Corbie and DeChance went in after him.

"Cheerful-looking place," said Corbie. "I take it you've noticed there are no other doorways in here? What happens if the door we just came through decides to disappear again?"

"Then you get to blow a hole in the wall. DeChance, are you all right?"

The marines moved a step closer to the esper as she swayed unsteadily on her feet. Her face was ghostly pale in the dim light, her eyes fixed and staring.

"I can hear them," she said faintly. "I can feel them, all around us. They're waking up."

"Who are?" said Corbie.

"They're waking up," said DeChance. "They're coming for us. They want what makes us sane."

CHAPTER FOUR

The Alien

"IF we're going to set a trap," said Investigator Krystel, "I have to be the bait. No offence, Captain, but I'm most likely to survive if something goes wrong."

"You'll get no argument from me," said Hunter. "I've seen an Investigator in action before."

"From a distance, I trust," said Krystel.

"Of course," said Hunter. "I'm still here, aren't I?"

Krystel smiled fleetingly and looked round the large open square they'd chosen as the setting for their trap. Jagged metallic buildings stood side by side with squat stone monoliths and intricate structures of spiked glass. There were only three entrances to the square, one of which was blocked with a high wall of rubble from a derelict building. There was no sign to show why the building had collapsed, and its neighbours seemed unaffected. Krystel eased her sword in its scabbard, and checked the power level on her force shield. Everything was ready. All they had to do now was bait the trap and stand ready to spring it.

It should work; it was simple and straightforward. Hunter and Williams would leave the square, making a great deal of noise as they did so, and then circle quietly back, staying under cover all the way. Krystel, on the other hand, would take her ease in the middle of the square, and wait to see if anything came to join her. Simple and straightforward. Krystel believed in being direct and to the point whenever possible. The more complicated a plan was, the more chances there were for something to go wrong. Besides, they were working against a deadline. They had only three hours or so before night fell, and none of them wanted to be caught in the city after dark. The city might be deserted, but its ghosts didn't feel at all friendly.

Hunter and Williams made loud good-byes, and left the square together. It seemed very quiet with them gone. Krystel walked over to the wall of rubble, sat down on a comfortable-looking stone slab, and took a cigar stub out of her pocket. She took her time about lighting it, trying hard to give the impression of being completely relaxed and at ease. Normally, she'd have thrown away a stub this small, but she'd nearly finished the pack she'd brought with her. Waste not, want not, as her mother used to say. Krystel drew her sword, took a piece of rag from the top of her boot, and polished the blade with long, easy strokes. The familiar ritual was quietly soothing. When the job was done, she put the piece of rag away and sat with the sword lying flat across her thighs. It was a good blade. A claymore, handed down through three generations of her family. She hoped she'd brought no dishonour to the sword, though sometimes she wasn't sure. An Investigator's work was like that, mostly.

She wondered idly what she'd be facing when the time came. The scale of the buildings meant it would be big, probably around nine to ten feet tall. She remembered the statues from the plain, frowned slightly, and then shrugged. It didn't matter. Whatever it was, she could handle it. She was an Investigator.

She sat up straight suddenly. A faint repetitive sound came clearly to her on the quiet. She looked quickly around her, but there was no trace of any movement, and she couldn't place which direction the sound was coming from. Krystel stubbed out her cigar and put what was left of it back in her pocket for later. She stood up, sword and disrupter in hand, and slapped her left wrist against her side. The glowing force shield appeared on her arm. She stood waiting, confident and ready, checking out possible cover and escape routes. Whatever was coming sounded large and heavy and determined, but the sounds echoed round and round the square until she couldn't tell where they originated. Captain Hunter and Dr. Williams should be somewhere close at hand by now, but she knew she couldn't afford to depend on them. The sound was drawing nearer. A long, wailing howl suddenly broke the silence, shrill and powerful and horribly angry. Krystel's hackles rose sharply. Something about the awful sound touched her deeply on some basic, primitive level, and she felt a sudden impulse to turn and run until she'd left the alien city far behind her. She crushed the thought ruthlessly. She was an Investigator, and it was just another alien.

Investigators killed aliens. That was their function, their reason for being.

She moved quickly into a shadowed alcove and set her back against the wall. The approaching footsteps were like thunder. The beast howled again, and for the first time Krystel caught a glimpse of something moving beyond the high wall of rubble. She raised her gun, and waited for a target. The rubble suddenly burst apart as the alien crashed through it. Shards of broken stone and metal flew through the air like jagged hail. The beast stepped out into the square, and Krystel's face screwed up in disgust.

It was tall, well over twenty feet. It would have been taller if it hadn't been for the stooping back and thrust-forward head. It was dirty white in colour, its rough hide more like scale than skin. It walked on two legs, and it looked something like a man. Great slabs of muscle corded and bunched on its huge form, but the proportions were somehow wrong. Disturbingly wrong. The twisted arms hung almost to the ground. One arm ended in a viciously clawed hand. The other erupted into a mass of writhing tentacles. Its face was a rigid mask of sharp-edged bone. The great snarling mouth was full of jagged teeth. There were two lidless eyes, yellow as urine, with no trace of pupil or retina. It lurched awkwardly forward into the square, as though searching for some sound or scent it couldn't quite detect.

Krystel had to fight down an urge to look away. It wasn't the alien's form, ugly though it was; she'd seen worse in her time. The alien's flesh was rotten and decaying, and it left a trail of foulness behind it. Nubs of discoloured bone showed through the splitting hide, which stretched and tore with every movement. In places, the flesh seemed to stir and writhe of its own volition, as though maggots seethed beneath the surface.

Krystel took a long, slow breath to steady herself, took careful aim with her disrupter, and pressed the stud. The beam of searing energy hit just above the creature's eyes, and the entire head exploded in a flurry of bloody flesh and bone. The alien slumped to its knees, fell on its side, and lay still. Krystel watched carefully to be sure it was dead, feeling almost let down. *Is that it?* she thought finally, holstering her gun. *All that planning and preparation, and the stupid creature went down under a single disrupter shot.* She smiled briefly. She should have known. Investigators killed aliens. That's just the way it was.

She stepped out of the alcove and walked unhurriedly across the square towards the unmoving alien. It was certainly big enough, even larger than she'd expected. Where the hell had it been hiding all this time? More importantly, how many more creatures like this were there, and where were they hiding? Hunter and Williams appeared from different sides of the square, guns in hand, and walked over to join her. Krystel looked thoughtfully at the dead alien. At twenty feet tall, it was probably the biggest thing she'd ever shot. Maybe she should have it stuffed and mounted as a trophy. She was about ten feet away when the alien suddenly lurched to its feet. It stood swaying for a moment, and then a new head thrust up from the bloody ruin of its neck. The eyes opened slowly, the eyelids parting stickily, and then its great mouth gaped wide as the alien's horrid voice echoed across the square.

Krystel grabbed for her gun, knowing even as she did so that the energy crystal hadn't had time to recharge yet. The alien whirled round to face her, and she brought her force shield up between them. The claymore was a solid weight in her hand. Close up, she could see the rotting flesh writhing and falling apart on the alien's body. The stench was appalling. It looked steadily at her with its dull yellow eyes, and its grinning mouth stretched impossibly wide. It was reaching for her with its clawed hand when two bolts of searing energy tore its neck and chest apart. Flesh and blood spattered against Krystel's shield, and she backed quickly away as the alien swung round to face the men who had hurt it. Already its shifting flesh was making good the gaping holes in its chest and throat. Hunter and Williams activated their force shields as the alien turned on them. The tentacles on the end of its right arm stretched impossibly as they reached for the two men.

"This way!" yelled Krystel, indicating with her sword the nearest of the escape routes she'd spotted earlier. She ran for the narrow passageway, and Hunter and Williams ran after her. The alien howled deafeningly and lurched after them. Krystel glanced back over her shoulder. The alien was already closing the gap, moving impossibly quickly for its bulk. Krystel ran full tilt down the passageway between the two buildings, Hunter and Williams sprinting after her, and tried to figure out where the hell to head for next. They weren't going to be able to outrun the creature. She needed somewhere they could make a stand.

She raked the buildings around her with a desperate glare, and then spotted an open doorway to her right. Without slowing her pace she changed direction, and raced for it. She charged through, gun and sword at the ready, but the gloomy chamber before her appeared to be deserted. Hunter and Williams crowded through after her, and the three of them looked quickly round for something they could use to block the doorway. The room was empty, save for a dozen or so gleaming metallic spirals hanging from the ceiling. Krystel spotted another doorway on the opposite side of the room and padded quickly over to peer into the shadowy opening. She gestured for Hunter and Williams to join her, and then stepped over the threshold.

The new room was even darker, but they didn't dare use a lantern. The alien might see it. They shut off their force shields, sat down with their backs to the wall, and waited for their eyes to adjust to the gloom. Everything was still and quiet; the only sound in the huge room was their own slowing breathing.

"I can't hear it anymore," said Williams. "Can you?"

"It's still out there," said Hunter. "It knows we can't have gone far."

"What the hell was it?" asked Williams. "I saw it die, and it got up again. It's like something out of legend. The undead, the beasts that cannot die . . ."

"Superstition is for immature minds," snapped Krystel. "Whatever that alien is, it's real enough. I've still got some of its blood on my uniform. And when I blew its head off, it took some time before it could recover enough to grow another. It can be hurt. Stunned."

"But can it be killed?" said Williams. "Or is it already dead? Its flesh was decaying . . . I know decomposing flesh when I see it!"

"Keep your voice down," said Hunter. "Do you want it to hear you?"

Williams shut up. Hunter leaned his head back against the wall and closed his eyes for a moment. There had to be a way out of this, if only he could think of it. He had to think of something; he was the Captain. It was his responsibility. It was a pity the pinnace was so far away. Its guns would have blown the alien into so many pieces, it would never have been able to put itself back together again. But he might as well wish for the moons. Even if he could summon the pinnace by remote control, by the time it reached the city everything would be over, one way or another. He looked at Krystel.

"Any comments, Investigator?"

"Our guns should have recharged by now," said Krystel. "Maybe if we all hit it with disrupters at the same time . . ."

"That sounds more like a last resort than a plan of action," said Hunter. "But for want of anything better I suppose it'll have to do."

"There's always the concussion grenades," said Williams.

"Not accurate enough. That thing can move bloody quickly when it puts its mind to it. Any other suggestions?"

"Retreat," said Krystel. "Get the hell out of the city and leave the alien behind. Most creatures have a strong sense of territory; if we put enough space between us and it, it should lose interest in us."

"That's a lot of ifs and maybes," said Williams. "You're supposed to be an expert on alien forms. Haven't you got anything definite you can tell us?"

"It's huge, it's angry, and it's dangerous," said Krystel. "It can regenerate damaged tissue. Our weapons are useless against it, and it will quite definitely kill us if we don't start acting intelligently. On the other hand, for all its power, it doesn't appear to be very bright. With its advantages, I suppose it doesn't have to be. But all the time we're sitting here arguing, it's getting closer. It could be here any minute."

Hunter closed his eyes and tried hard to concentrate. There had to be a way out of this.

"If it was going to come straight in here after us, it would have been here by now," he said finally. "So what's stopping it?"

Krystel shrugged. "I can't advise you, Captain. I don't have enough information. Normally, with a new species like this I'd spend months checking it out from a distance, before even thinking of approaching it."

She broke off as Williams suddenly sat up straight. "It's entered the building," he said flatly. "I can hear it."

Hunter held his breath and listened, but couldn't hear anything. He looked at Krystel, who shrugged slightly. Hunter bit his lip. More of the good doctor's hidden augmentations, presumably. Williams stirred restlessly.

"We can't just sit here in the dark, Captain. We've got to do something."

"Keep your voice down," said Krystel. "We don't know how good its hearing is. And there's no point in just running blindly."

"There's no point in just waiting here for the damned thing to find us! Captain, we've got to get out of here!"

There was a sudden stench of corruption, and the room was suddenly darker as the alien's bulk loomed up outside the huge doorway. Its horrid roar was deafening in the confined space.

"Disrupters!" yelled Hunter, as the three of them scrambled to their feet. "Aim for the head!"

The three disrupters fired almost as one, and the alien's head blew apart. But this time, the creature didn't fall. It braced itself on its massive legs and groped blindly through a doorway for its attackers. The three of them backed quickly away, holstering their guns and activating their force shields. Krystel drew her claymore and hacked at the writhing tentacles as they reached for her face. The blade cut cleanly through the rotten flesh, but the wounds healed themselves in seconds. A new head burst up out of the bloody mess of its neck. Its yellow eyes shone in the darkness.

Hunter swung his sword with all his strength, and the blade sliced through the shifting white flesh and out again, without leaving a wound. The alien cut at Hunter with its clawed hand, and he put up his force shield between them. The impact of the blow sent him staggering backwards. Krystel yelled at the beast to get its attention, and when it turned on her she sliced at its arm with the edge of her shield. The glowing energy field sheared clean through the wrist, severing the clawed hand. It fell to the floor, the fingers still curling and uncurling. The claws dug furrows in the floor. A pale blood spurted from the stump. The alien screamed, and batted at Krystel with its injured arm. The Investigator threw herself to one side. The blow barely clipped her in passing, but she was still slammed against the wall. Hunter grabbed her before her knees could buckle, but she quickly got her breath back and shrugged him off.

"There's another doorway on the far side of the room!" she shouted. "Take Williams and get out of here. I'll hold the creature back to give you a start. I'll join you as soon as I can. Now move it!"

Williams turned and ran for the other doorway, and Hunter reluctantly followed him. Krystel had to know what she was doing. She was an Investigator.

The alien forced its massive body through the doorway, wrecking the surrounding wall in the process. Krystel moved in close and hacked at the beast with her claymore and shield, her mouth stretched in a tight and nasty grin, her eyes gleaming with a killing fever. The alien howled endlessly, its wailing voice almost unbearable at close range. The sheer fury of Krystel's attack held the alien where it was, but its wounds healed in seconds, and even through her killing rage, Krystel knew she wasn't really hurting it. She snarled once into its grinning face, and then turned and ran. The alien lurched after her, but she was already across the room and plunging through the far doorway by the time it had started to build up speed. Hunter and Williams were waiting for her at the base of a tall tower. A ramp led up the side of the wall into darkness.

"This way!" said Hunter. "There's no other choice. If nothing else, this should put some space between us and the creature. Move it!"

He led the way up the ramp, with Williams and Krystel crowding close behind. After a while, they calmed down enough to turn off their force shields, to save energy. The steep slope made the going hard, and Hunter's thighs were soon aching fiercely. He drove himself on regardless, and snarled at the others when they looked like slowing. He couldn't hear the alien yet, but he had no doubt it was still on their trail. He held his field lantern out before him, its golden light illuminating the tower above and below him. He watched his feet carefully; as before, there was no safety rail, and a slip at the wrong moment could easily prove fatal. The tower seemed to go on forever, and the drop just kept getting longer. He scowled into the gloom ahead. How the hell could everything have gone wrong so quickly? Doors came and went in the wall beside him, but he kept pressing on. He could hear the alien coming up the ramp after them. It was getting closer.

And finally they ran out of ramp. Bright light fell through an open doorway, and Hunter had no choice but to plunge into it. He lurched to a halt as the brilliant sunlight blinded him, and he blinked painfully for several moments before his sight returned. He turned off his field lantern and put it back in his backpack as he looked quickly around him.

Huge, enigmatic structures covered the length and breadth of the roof, dwarfing Hunter and his companions. The towering shapes were complex and bizarre, composed of a pearly iridescent material that softened and distorted every detail until they passed beyond meaning and into mystery. Hunter stared silently about him, unable to react at all. They were too bewildering, too alien, for any reaction of his to make sense. They were beyond any rational or emotional response. They simply were, and Hunter couldn't tear his eyes away from them.

"Fascinating," said Krystel. "I wonder what they do?"

Her voice broke the spell, and Hunter shook his head, disorientated. "Save the questions for another day," he said finally. "That creature will be here any minute. Start looking for a way off this roof."

"Wait a minute," said Williams unexpectedly. "I have a problem. I can't seem to raise the pinnace computers."

Hunter looked at him blankly for a moment, and then activated his own comm implant. He reached out for the computers, but there was nothing there; only silence. It was like reaching out in the dark for a light switch and finding only empty space. Hunter swallowed hard. He'd known that one day he'd have to learn to do without the computers, but the sudden silence had caught him unprepared. "Investigator, Williams; can you hear me?"

"Not through my comm unit," said Krystel. "We're cut off, Captain."

"We've got to get back to the pinnace," said Williams urgently. "We've got to re-establish contact. All my work, all my memories are there!"

"One thing at a time, Doctor," said Hunter. "First, we get off the roof; then we'll decide what to do next."

"Quiet!" said Krystel. "The creature's almost here." She moved over to the doorway, pulled a concussion grenade from her bandolier, primed it, and tossed it down the ramp. She backed quickly away, and the tower shook as the grenade exploded some distance below.

"That should slow it down," said Krystel. She looked at Hunter. "There's only one way of this roof, Captain, and we both know what it is. The bridges."

She gestured at the gossamer metal strands that hung between the tower and its surrounding buildings, and Hunter winced.

"I was afraid you were going to say that. I don't trust those things. They look as though they'd blow away in a good wind."

"The aliens must have used them," said Williams. "And they weigh a hell of a lot more than we do."

Hunter looked at the webbing again, and then back at the doorway. "All right; let's do it. And quickly, before I get a rush of brains to the head and realise how crazy this is."

He moved over to the edge of the roof, hesitated briefly, and then sat down and swung his legs out and over onto the webbing. He looked down once, and decided not to do that again. It was a long way down. He muttered something indistinct, even to himself, and stepped gingerly out onto the bridge. It was six to seven feet wide, a tangled mess of grey strands barely an inch or so in diameter. There were no handrails. The threads gave slightly under his weight, but held. Hunter gritted his teeth, and sheathed his sword and gun so as to have both hands free. He walked steadily forward, carefully not looking down or back, and kept his gaze fixed on the building ahead. It didn't seem to be getting any closer. At the back of his mind, he couldn't help wondering if the webbing had been spun by a machine, or some gigantic creature. The bridge rippled and shook as Williams and Krystel followed him, but it seemed to be holding all their weight well enough. Hunter began to relax a little.

They hadn't got far when the bridge lurched sickly to one side. Hunter fell to one knee and grabbed at the strands for support. He looked back, past Williams and Krystel, already knowing what he was going to see. The alien had found them. It snarled soundlessly, exposing its jagged teeth, and made its way steadily along the bridge towards them. The bridge bounced and swayed, but the fragile-looking gossamer threads held the creature's weight easily. Hunter swore under his breath and rose unsteadily to his feet.

"Investigator, take the doctor and get to the next building. I'll hold the alien back. If I don't join you, find the others and tell them what's happened. Then get the hell out of this city, and back to the pinnace. Yell for help, and keep on yelling till you get it. That's it. No arguments. Move."

Williams pushed past him and ran down the bridge. Krystel stayed where she was. "I should stay, not you. I'm the Investigator."

"That's why you have to go, Krystel. They're going to need you."

"We need you."

"No one's needed me for a long time. I'm not reliable anymore. Now will you please get the hell out of here?"

Krystel nodded briefly, and hurried after Williams. Hunter watched her go for a moment, and then turned to face the oncoming alien. It looked bigger than he remembered. Its rotting white flesh seemed to slip and slide on its frame, but the teeth in the grinning mouth looked horribly efficient. Hunter drew his gun. He didn't have to look down to know his hand was shaking. His stomach ached from the tension and sweat was pouring off him. Yet scared as he was, terrified as he was, he wasn't panicking. His mind was clear. He knew what he had to do and he was ready to do it. Maybe that was all he'd really needed—a simple, straightforward certainty in his life, something he could understand and cling to.

The alien was nearly upon him. He could smell it on the air, hear its panting breath. There was no point in trying to shoot it. They'd tried that and it hadn't worked. His sword and force shield would be less than useless. The creature had already grown a new hand to replace the one Krystel had cut off. And he couldn't turn and run. The alien would soon catch him and kill him, and then it would go after Krystel and Williams. No. Hunter took a firm grip on his gun, and his hand steadied. He had to buy time for the others, time for them to get away and warn the Empire about the nightmare on Wolf IV.

He'd always wondered where he would die. Upon what alien world, under what alien sun. He smiled once at the approaching alien, took careful aim with his disrupter, and blew out the bridge between them. The gossamer threads parted in a second under the searing energy, and the alien screamed shrilly as it fell, twisting and turning, to the street far below.

Hunter brushed against a flailing strand of webbing as he fell, and he dropped his sword and gun to grab at it with both hands. The webbing slid through his fingers as though it were greased. He tightened his grip till his hands ached, and finally got a firm hold on the strand. The sudden lurch as his fall was brought to a halt almost wrenched his arms from their sockets, but somehow he held on. The broken length of webbing swung downwards, its speed increasing as Hunter's weight pulled at it. The wall of the building opposite came flying towards him like a fly swatter. Hunter had a split-second glimpse of an open window looming up before him, and then the webbing slapped flat against the side of the building, hurling him through the window. He tried to hang on to his strand of webbing, but it was wrenched from his hands. He curled into a ball instinctively, then crashed into something hard but yielding, which gave under the impact. Hunter careered on, unable to stop, and smashed through another barrier. All the breath was knocked from his lungs, and the pain was so bad he blacked out.

He came back to consciousness slowly, in fits and starts. For a long while all he could do was lie on his back and stare at the ceiling. And that was how Krystel and Williams found him. They forced their way through the wreckage that half-filled the room, and made their way over to Hunter. Williams knelt beside him and checked him over with brisk efficiency. Hunter grinned up at Krystel.

"What happened to the alien?"

"Hit the ground and spattered," said Krystel succinctly. "We'll be lucky to find any pieces big enough to study."

Hunter wanted to laugh, but his ribs hurt too much. He sat up slowly, with Williams' help, and looked around.

"From the look of it, this room was full of partitions," said Krystel. "Emphasis on the word *was*. You seem to have demolished most of them."

"Good thing you did," said Williams. "They absorbed most of your speed and impact. The fall would have killed you otherwise. You're lucky to be alive, Captain."

"Don't think I don't know it," said Hunter. He nodded to Williams to let go of him, and stood swaying for a moment while his head settled. "How bad is the damage, Doctor?"

"Extensive bruising, and some lacerations. You could have a cracked rib or two, not to mention concussion. I really think we should get back to the pinnace so I can check you over properly."

"For once, I think I agree with you, Doctor." Hunter rubbed tiredly at his aching forehead. "As long as there was a chance the city was deserted, I could justify checking it out ourselves, but the alien changes all that. We have to contact the Empire."

"That could mean a delay in the arrival of the colonists," said Williams.

"Yes," said Hunter. "I know." He looked at Krystel. "I don't suppose you found any trace of my gun and my sword? I dropped them."

"I'm afraid not, Captain," said the Investigator. "But you're welcome to use my disrupter. I've always preferred the sword, myself. It's more personal."

Hunter took the gun from her with a nod of thanks, and slipped it into his holster. "All right, the first thing is to contact the rest of the Squad. They should have reached the city by now."

"There's always the chance they encountered one of the aliens themselves," said Krystel. "They might not have been as fortunate as us."

"You're right." Hunter scowled for a moment. "We'll head for the copper tower, just in case my last message to them got through. If they're not there, we'll have to give up on them for now and get back to the pinnace. The Empire must be warned."

"Yes," said Krystel. "The last time I came up against an alien this hard to kill was on Grendel."

Slowly and cautiously, the three of them made their way down the winding ramp and out of the building. They were alert for any sound or movement, but the building was silent as a tomb. Every room they passed held strange shapes and machinery, but there was no sign of life anywhere. By the time they got out onto the street, the day was nearly over. Shadows were growing longer as the day darkened, and the turquoise sky held veins of red from the sinking sun.

"It'll be night soon," said Williams quietly. "I don't think we should spend a night in the city, Captain. There's no telling what might roam the streets once the sun goes down."

"We can't just abandon the others," said Hunter. "They're part of the Squad."

"We can if we have to," said Krystel. "They're expendable. Just like us."

Evening fell across the city. The street was filled with shadows, and strange lights burned brightly in open windows. And in the dark, hidden heart of the city, something awful slowly grew stronger.

✢

CHAPTER FIVE

The Prey

LINDHOLM led the way down the deserted street, gun in hand, alert for any sign of life or movement. Corbie followed close behind, hurrying the esper along as best he could. DeChance's face was smooth and blank, empty of all emotion or personality. Her eyes saw nothing, and she walked uncaringly wherever Corbie led her. The marine scowled, as much in worry as anger. DeChance had been acting brainburned ever since she made mental contact with something in the city.

They're waking up, she'd said. *They're coming for us. They want what makes us sane.*

She hadn't said a word after that. The light went out of her eyes, and she could no longer hear the marines, no matter how loudly they shouted. Her face became gaunt and drawn, and she only moved when the marines guided her. At first they thought her condition might have been caused by the building they were in, but even after they'd hustled her outside she remained lost and silent. Corbie had pressed for them to keep moving. If there was something coming after them, they'd be better off presenting a moving target. Lindholm reluctantly agreed, and led the way. Corbie let him. Right now, he needed somebody else to be in charge, to do his thinking for him.

He glanced quickly around. They were walking between two massive structures of crystal and metal fused together, so tall that Corbie had to tilt back his head to see the top of them. There were no lights in any of the windows, and the only sound on the quiet was the soft, steady padding of their own footsteps. There'd been no sign of any living

thing since the esper's warning, but still Corbie's back felt
the pressure of unseen watching eyes.

He tried to imagine something so terrible that just mental
contact with it could destroy your mind, and couldn't. The
fear was with him always now, trembling in his hands,
burning in his eyes. His stomach was a tight knot of pain.
He tried to concentrate on where they were heading, to
keep his mind occupied, but all he knew for sure was the
name the esper had given it. The copper tower. Corbie
sniffed unhappily and scowled about him, trying to get
his bearings. He'd been turned around so much he wasn't
even sure where the boundaries were anymore. Lindholm
was still striding purposefully ahead of him, though, so
presumably at least he knew where they were going.

"How long since you tried the comm unit?" said Lindholm
suddenly, his voice calm and quiet as always.

"Maybe ten minutes. Want me to try again?"

"Sure. Give it a try."

Corbie activated his comm implant. "Captain, this is
Corbie. Please respond." He waited several moments, but
there was no answer, only the unnerving silence, empty
even of static. He tried twice more, and then gave up.
Lindholm said nothing.

DeChance suddenly stumbled, and almost fell. Corbie
had to support all her weight for a moment, and then her
back straightened as she found her feet again. She shook
her head dazedly, and made a few meaningless noises
with her mouth. Corbie looked at Lindholm, and motioned
urgently towards the nearest building. Lindholm nodded.
Between the two of them, the marines got DeChance over
to the open doorway. It was set in the side of a gleaming
pearlescent dome, a hundred feet high or more. There were
no windows or other openings, only the smooth, featureless
surface of the dome. Lindholm went through the doorway
first, gun at the ready, his force shield blazing on his arm.
Corbie gave him a moment and then guided the esper in
after him.

Inside, there was only darkness. There was a flash of
light as Lindholm lit his field lantern, and the room came

into being around them. It was roughly thirty feet square, with a low ceiling. The walls and ceiling were both strangely curved in places, and shone a dull silver-grey in the lantern light. Lindholm put the lantern down on the floor then went to give Corbie a hand with the esper. DeChance sat down suddenly on the floor, as though all the strength had gone out of her legs. Corbie helped her lean back against the nearest wall. It felt warm and spongelike to the touch, and Corbie glared at it suspiciously before turning his attention back to DeChance.

"I think this may have been a mistake," said Lindholm suddenly. "I don't like the feel of this place."

"You took the words right out of my mouth," said Corbie. "Unfortunately, the esper's in no condition to travel any further."

"How is she?"

"I'm not sure. She might be coming out of it. Then again . . ."

"Yeah." Lindholm looked quickly around him. There was a wide opening in the far wall, full of darkness. "We can't stay here, Russ. We can't even barricade the doorway. Get her on her feet again, and we'll see what's back of this room. You bring the lantern."

He moved warily towards the open doorway, while Corbie grabbed the field lantern with one hand, and urged DeChance to her feet with the other. The esper was still dazed, but at least now she was cooperating with him.

"Come on, Russ," said Lindholm impatiently. "It's not safe here."

"Safe? I haven't felt safe since we landed on this bloody planet. If you're in such a hurry, how about giving me a hand? The esper isn't getting any lighter to lug around, you know."

Lindholm took the lantern away from him, and held it up to light the next room. Corbie glared at Lindholm's back, and then peered through the open doorway. The room was huge. The shadows beyond the light made it impossible to judge its true size, but once again Corbie was struck by the sheer scale of the alien city. He felt like a child who'd escaped from the nursery and wandered into the part of the world where the adults lived. The curving walls were a dull reddish colour in the lantern light, marked here and there by sharp-edged protrusions. The floor was cracked and split apart, like mud that had dried out under a midday sun. The room itself was quite empty. Lindholm moved slowly forward and Corbie followed him, still half-supporting the esper. The far wall suddenly became clear as the lantern light moved, and Corbie scowled unhappily. Spurs of metal jutted from the crimson wall, like the horns of forgotten beasts. For a moment Corbie wondered if they could be trophies of some kind, and immediately the walls seemed to him to be exactly the color of dried blood. A round opening in the wall yawned like a toothless mouth.

"Where are we?" said DeChance hoarsely, and Corbie jumped.

"It's all right," he said quickly. "You're quite safe. We're inside one of the buildings. It's empty. How do you feel?"

"I'm not sure. Strange." She shook her head slowly. "There were so many traces, so many alien minds, I just got lost among them. I couldn't understand any of them. Their thought patterns made no sense." Her face cleared suddenly, losing all its vagueness, and she looked sharply at the two marines. "We've got to get out of the city. If there's one thing I am sure of, it's that they're dangerous. Horribly dangerous."

"You keep saying *they*," said Lindholm. "How many aliens are there? Where are they hiding?"

"They're here," said DeChance. "They're all around. Waiting. They've been waiting a very long time. We woke them up. I don't know how many there are; hundreds, thousands. I don't know. The traces kept shifting, changing. But they're close. I know that. They're getting closer all the time. We've got to get out of the city."

"Sounds good to me," said Corbie. "Sven?"

"Hold on a minute, Russ." Lindholm looked thoughtfully at the esper. "No offence, DeChance, but just how reliable is what you've been telling us? Are you giving us facts or impressions?"

"Both. Neither. I can't explain esp to anyone who isn't an esper. Contact with an alien mind is difficult; they don't think like we do. It's like looking in a distorted mirror, trying to find things you recognise. I managed to pick up a few things I'm sure of. The power sources for the city are all underground, buried deep in the bedrock. They go down for miles. They're still functioning, despite being abandoned for centuries. Now the city's coming alive, and drawing more and more power. I don't know what the power's for, but it's got something to do with the copper tower in the centre of the city. That tower is the key to everything that's happening here."

"Then we'd better go and take a look at it," said Lindholm. "Maybe we'll find a few answers there."

"Are you crazy?" said Corbie. "You heard the esper; this whole place is coming alive, and hundreds, maybe thousands of monsters are heading our way right now! We've got to get out of here while we still can!"

"Come on, Russ; we can't just walk away from this. We have a responsibility to the rest of the Squad, and the colonists who'll come after us. This is our best chance to get some answers, while everything's still waking up and disorientated."

"Responsibility? Sven, they dumped us here to die. No one gives a damn about us. We're expendable; that's why they sent us. Our only responsibility is to ourselves."

"What about the rest of the Squad?"

"What about them?"

"Allow me," said DeChance to Lindholm. "Corbie, much as I hate to admit it, Sven's right. If we don't find the answers now, while we've got a chance, the aliens in this city will kill us all. They'll roll right over us. We can't leave. Our only hope is the copper tower, and what we might find there. Now shut up and soldier."

Corbie nodded glumly. "Some days you just shouldn't get out of bed. All right, esper; how far is it to the tower?"

"Not far. A mile, at most."

"Do you feel up to travelling that far?"

"I think so."

"Anything else we need to know about the tower?" said Lindholm.

"Yes." DeChance frowned, her eyes vague and far away. "I think it's insane."

"Great," said Corbie. "Just great."

Lindholm had just started to nod agreement when the room suddenly came alive around them. Blurred shapes thrust up out of the floor, grey and white and beaded with sweat. The marines moved quickly to stand back to back, guns at the ready. A new light pierced the darkness as they raised their force shields. DeChance raised hers a moment later, and moved in close beside the marines, gun and sword in hand. More growths burst out of the walls. Somewhere far away, something was shrieking with what might have been rage or pain or both. The growths blossomed out into huge mushroom shapes, with wide, drooping heads on long, waving stalks. Crude eyes appeared on the stalks, and the fluted edges of the flat heads fluttered with the steady rhythm of slow breathing. The growths sprouted from every side, spreading out to fill the room.

Corbie yelled out in surprise as a mushroom blossomed out of the floor at his feet, and he fired his disrupter at it. The fleshy head exploded under the energy bolt. The stalk swayed back and forth for a moment, and then a dozen flailing tentacles erupted out of the stalk, lashing furiously at the air. They were bloodred, and tipped with tiny sucking mouths. Corbie cut at them with his sword, but for every tentacle he severed, another burst out of the stalk to take its place. Lindholm looked from the doorway to the opening in the far wall and tried to work out which was the nearest. He had a sinking feeling the nearest opening was the one that led deeper into the building. One of the mushroom growths leaned towards him, top-heavy on its slender stalk, and Lindholm only just managed to stop himself from firing at it. He didn't want to repeat Corbie's mistake. The centre of the bowed mushroom head bulged suddenly outwards, and then split apart as a huge black-armoured insect exploded out of it. It had a wide, flat body, a dozen barbed legs, and razor-sharp mandibles. It reached hungrily for Lindholm, and he shot it at point-blank range. The armoured body blew apart, twitching legs flying through the air.

All over the room, the mushroom growths were swelling up and bursting open, giving birth to monsters. Corbie and Lindholm holstered their guns and tried to clear a space around them with their swords. The esper was no use to them. Her gun hung slackly at her side, her face drawn and twisted by some inner agony. The marines protected her as best they could, but they both knew they couldn't do that for long. There were just too many monsters.

A huge mushroom head exploded, throwing hundreds of bloodred worms across the room. They fell upon monsters and mushrooms alike, and began to chew voraciously through whatever they landed on. The marines were mostly protected by their force shields and steelmesh tunics, but still a few landed on bare flesh. One worm landed on Lindholm's hand, and bit clear through to the bone before he could shake it off. He cursed briefly, and kept on fighting. In the Arenas you learned to ignore any wound that wasn't immediately critical. Corbie wasn't nearly so calm about it, and shrieked and cursed at the top of his voice when a worm attached itself to his ear. He clawed desperately at the worm with his free hand, and in tearing it off almost decapitated himself with his own force shield. Several worms landed on the esper, shocking her out of her trance, and she brushed and slapped frantically at them where they clung to her uniform. The monsters ignored the worms in their single-minded determination to reach their human prey. A long, dull grey tentacle snapped out of nowhere and grabbed Lindholm's field lantern. The lantern shattered in its grip, and the light winked out. The room was still lit by an eerie, ghostly glow from the mushrooms, but it was rapidly being blocked out by the growing horde of monsters.

The marines fought on, despite the growing ache in their backs and arms and the air that burned in their straining lungs. DeChance protected them with her force shield as best she could, but she was no fighter, and they all knew it. Huge armoured insects up to three and four feet in length crawled over the floor and walls, and fought each other for the chance to get at their human prey. Long tentacles studded with snapping mouths thrashed the air. Something broken-backed with too many legs crawled upside down across the ceiling, watching the marines with unblinking eyes. The worms were everywhere, writhing and coiling and eating. Corbie wiped sweat from his eyes with the back of his hand, and something with foot-long teeth snapped at his throat. He got his force shield up just in time, and the teeth broke jaggedly against the energy field. He could feel the strength going out of him with each of his sword thrusts, but he kept fighting anyway. He had to. There was nowhere to retreat. He couldn't even see the doorway anymore. He grinned defiantly, and swung his sword in short, vicious arcs while he waited for his disrupter to recharge. A mushroom burst out of the wall beside him, and as he cut through the stem, a writhing mass of intestines fell out of the wound, smoking and steaming on the still air.

Right, thought Corbie determinedly. *That is it. Enough is enough.*

He cleared some space around him with his sword and shield, lifted his gun, and blasted a hole through the nearest wall. DeChance and Lindholm quickly used their guns to blast a path through the crowding monsters, and the three of them clambered through the hole into the darkness beyond. The two marines turned and blocked the gap with their force shields while DeChance pulled her field lantern out of her backpack. The sudden flare of light showed the room was empty, apart from some alien machinery, and the esper relaxed a little. Monsters pressed against the two force shields, trying to force their way past. A mushroom head exploded, blowing a hail of writhing maggots into the air.

"We've got to block this hole off and barricade it," said Lindholm. His breath was coming in short, ragged pants, but his voice was as calm and unconcerned as always.

"Sounds good to me," said Corbie. "You and the esper find something. I'll hold them off. But you'd better be bloody quick."

He stepped forward to fill the hole, somehow finding some last reserves of strength to draw on. The monsters surged forward, and he met them with his sword and shield. Tired and aching and preoccupied as he was, Corbie still found time to notice he wasn't as frightened as he had been. He was still scared, but it wasn't the heart-stopping, paralysing fear that had bedevilled him for so long. He was scared, but he could still think and he could still fight. Perhaps it was simply that he no longer had the choice of whether to fight or run. Being weak and indecisive here would simply get him killed. Not that Corbie had any illusions about his chances. Unless Sven or the esper came up with a miracle pretty damn quickly, he was a dead man, and he knew it. The thought twisted his stomach and shortened his breath, but it was no longer enough to paralyse him or break his nerve.

Who knows; maybe I'm just getting used to being terrified. . . .

His mouth stretched into a death's-head grin, and his gun blasted a creeping thing into a hundred twitching pieces.

"Move back out of the way, Russ! Now!"

Corbie fell back, and Lindholm single-handedly slammed a massive piece of alien machinery into the gap, sealing the hole off. Corbie didn't even want to think how much the damned thing must weigh. Certainly it looked strong enough to hold back the monsters while he and his companions made their escape. He started to move away from the wall, and collapsed. His vision darkened, and his head went muzzy.

"Easy, Russ," said Lindholm quickly. "Take a moment and get your second wind. The barricade will hold a while yet."

Corbie sat on the floor and concentrated on breathing deeply. His head was already clearing, but he could tell he wasn't up to running any distance yet, even assuming he had anywhere to run to. He glanced quickly around the new room. It wasn't quite as big as the last one, but even so, the lantern's light didn't carry to the far wall, and the high ceiling was hidden in shadow. Squat, hulking machinery stood in neat rows, no two the same. There were no lights or other signs to show they were still functioning. Corbie distrusted them anyway, on general principles. There was a jagged hole in the floor, its edges glowing-hot from an energy burst where Lindholm had used his disrupter to break a machine free from the floor. Lengths of steel and glass protruded from the hole like broken bones. Corbie took a deep breath, turned off his force shield, and got back on his feet again, with a little help from Lindholm and the esper.

"All right," he said hoarsely. "What now?"

Lindholm shrugged. "We can't go back, so we go on. There's another doorway, beyond the machines."

Corbie looked at DeChance. She had turned away, and was frowning distractedly, listening to something only she could hear.

"Well?" said Corbie finally. "What do you think, esper? Do you agree?"

"Yes," said DeChance. Her expression didn't change. "There's no other choice. All the other ways are blocked. Besides, there's something up ahead I want to look at."

Lindholm looked at her sharply. "What is it, esper? What's up ahead?"

"Something interesting," said DeChance dreamily. She turned her back on the two marines, and walked steadily between the alien machines to the far doorway. Corbie and Lindholm looked at each other briefly, and hurried after her. Corbie still didn't trust DeChance's esp, but it had proved accurate enough so far. And it beat standing around arguing next to a room full of monsters. He glared suspiciously at the alien machines as he passed, but they remained silent and enigmatic. They were structures with shape and form but no meaning. Or, at least, no meaning he could understand.

DeChance stepped through the open doorway, and held up her field lantern to illuminate the room. Corbie and Lindholm crowded in after her. The walls curved upwards to a shadowed ceiling far above. The room stretched away beyond the lantern's light, which gleamed dully on the endless ranks of metal stacks that filled the room like a honeycomb. And there, in those stacks, in that honeycomb, lay thousands upon thousands of milky white spheres, ranging in size from a man's fist to a man's head.

"They look like that ball you found in the monolith," said Lindholm. "What are they?"

"Memories," said DeChance softly. "A storehouse of memories. The history of this city, and those who lived here. The answers to all our questions."

She started towards the nearest stacks, but Lindholm grabbed her by the arm and made her stop. "Wait just a minute, esper. Remember the way you reacted to one of those things back in the monolith. There's no telling what these might do to you."

"Right," said Corbie. "And the monsters could be here any minute. We've got to keep moving."

"No," said DeChance flatly. "We need the information in these spheres. Without it, we don't have a hope in hell of surviving."

Lindholm nodded reluctantly, and let go of her arm. "All right. Russ, you look for another way out of here, while I stand guard. And DeChance, keep it short. We really don't have much time."

The esper nodded, her eyes fixed hungrily on the stacks and the spheres they held. Somewhere in that endless honeycomb lay the answers she needed; answers that would make sense of the insanity that threatened them. She walked slowly forward, wandering through the towering stacks with only her esp to guide her. All around her, the spheres burned in her mind like so many candles guttering in the darkness. They were old, very old, and their memories were fading. But a few still burned bright, flaring and brilliant, and DeChance's esp led her to them. She stretched out her hands.

At first there was only a colourless grey, like a monitor tuned to an empty channel, and then the first images came to her, like single frames from a moving film. DeChance's reason staggered under the impact. The alienness of the images was almost overpowering, but slowly DeChance forced sense and meaning out of them. And so the story unfolded before her, of a great race who dreamed a wonderful dream, and saw it collapse into a nightmare without end.

The aliens of Wolf IV had developed a strange and marvellous science, and used it to free themselves from the tyranny of a fixed shape. No longer bound to a single, rigid form, their physical shapes became a matter of choice. Their lives became free and wonderful. They grew wings and flew upon the wind. They adapted their bodies and burrowed through the earth. They soared above the atmosphere, and dived into volcanoes to swim in the molten lava. They were lords of creation, masters of all they surveyed.

But the change had not been natural. It was brought about and sustained by a single great device housed in a copper tower in the centre of the city. And slowly, horribly, the aliens learned the truth of what they had done to themselves. The shape of the body was controlled by the mind, and the aliens had forgotten there was more to the mind than the conscious will and the intellect. Body changes began to appear that were dictated by the demons of the subconscious mind, the id, the ego, and the superego; the dark areas of the mind, beyond sanity or hope of control. The aliens discovered hideous pleasures and awful longings, and their dreams became dark and foul. The horror had begun.

The aliens had been low-level telepaths, but the device changed all that. Their esp became wild and strong, and their minds were no longer sacrosanct. They quickly learned that the more powerful mind could overpower the weaker, and force a change upon the loser's body. Before the great device, the aliens of Wolf IV had been a calm, thoughtful people. They lived long, and delighted in the act of creation. But they had reached too far and lost everything they prized, and in the end only monsters remained to stalk the city streets.

The city fell. Its streets were purulent with awful life, madness given shape and form. And so they came to the final horror. The aliens could not die. If a limb was torn away, it grew back. A wound would heal itself in seconds. The monsters tore and ate each other, but even the worst atrocities could not kill them now.

The city survived for a while. The device only affected living, animate matter. But eventually the city fell apart as the machines went untended. Only the great device, built to be self-perpetuating, continued in its purpose. Its influence spread across the planet, affecting all that lived, to some degree. But then something happened, something unforeseen.

The great device and the aliens had a continuing two-way contact, so that the device's programming could reflect the aliens' changing needs. And slowly, progressively, the aliens' madness began to drive the device insane. Its programming became warped and twisted as it struggled to fulfill the aliens' needs and desires. Finally, it recognised the danger it was in, and took the only course open to it. The device shut itself down and put the city to sleep, in the hope that the future might hold an answer to its dilemma.

Time passed. There was no telling how many years or centuries. The aliens could not die, and the device was patient. It waited, sustaining itself with the bare minimum of energy.

And then the Hell Squad came, and DeChance's esp roused the great device from its ancient sleep. But too much time had passed, and the device was no longer sane. Perhaps it had spent too long exposed to the aliens' madness, or perhaps simply the world had changed too much from the one it had been designed to serve, so that nothing made any sense to it anymore. It didn't matter. The great device had its programming.

It awoke the Sleepers and roused the city, and the nightmare began again.

DeChance fell to her knees, shaking uncontrollably. Corbie reached out a hand to steady her, only to hesitate as the esper vomited onto the floor. Lindholm looked back the way they'd come. Something was drawing near. He raised his force shield and drew his disrupter from its holster. The wall to their left suddenly cracked from top to bottom and burst apart as a huge armoured form crashed through it. A piece of flying stone smashed DeChance's field lantern, and darkness filled the room.

CHAPTER SIX

The Hunt

IT was evening, heading into night, as Hunter led Dr. Williams and the Investigator through the deserted city streets. The green of the sky grew dark and ominous as the sun sank slowly behind the cyclopean towers. The alien buildings cast strangely shaped shadows, and the occasional lighted window seemed bright and sinister in the deepening gloom. It was bitter cold and getting colder, and Hunter shivered despite the heating elements in his uniform. He glanced surreptitiously at Krystel and Williams, but neither of them showed any sign of being bothered by the cold. Hunter scowled. Investigators were trained to withstand extreme changes in temperature, but the doctor was just a civilian. Presumably those hidden adjustments of his made the difference. Hunter shared the popular distrust of black-market implants, but he had to admit there were times when they came in handy. He breathed on his freezing hands and beat them together, and tried to think warm thoughts.

They'd been walking for the best part of an hour, but the copper tower didn't seem to be drawing any nearer. It stood before them, tall and forbidding, rising high above the surrounding buildings, its gleaming metal spikes stark and jagged. It had seemed huge enough when they first started towards it, but now Hunter was beginning to realise just how tall and massive the structure really was. Not for the first time, he wondered what the hell he was going to do when he finally got there. If he got there.

Hunter let his hand fall to the disrupter at his side. He hadn't felt entirely happy about taking the Investigator's gun, after he lost his own, but he had to admit he felt a lot happier knowing he had a weapon to hand. And if half the things he'd heard about Investigators were true, she might not need a gun, at that. Williams still had both his gun and his sword, of course. Logically, he should have given up his sword so that Hunter could use it, since the doctor had no experience with a blade, but Hunter had decided against pressing the point. Williams was jumpy enough as it was; without his weapons to lend him courage he might just fall apart, for all his precious augmentations.

"Captain," said Williams suddenly. "I've been thinking . . ."

"Yes, Doctor," said Hunter politely.

"Our weapons weren't much use against that alien. In the future, if we come across anything else like that, why don't we just set up our portable force screen, and use that to protect us?"

Hunter felt like sighing deeply, but rose above it. "You must have noticed, Doctor, that it takes quite some time to set up a screen. I can't see the alien waiting patiently while we do it, can you? And even if we could get the screen up before the alien could get to us, what would we do then? Just sit tight, and wait for it to lose interest and go away? No, Doctor, as a plan it's not very practical. We'd do better to save the power in the screen's energy crystals for real emergencies."

He broke off as he realised the doctor wasn't listening to him. Williams scowled, bit his lower lip, and stopped dead in his tracks. Hunter and Krystel stopped with him. Williams looked slowly around him, his head cocked slightly to one side, as though listening to something only he could hear. Hunter listened, but everything seemed still and silent. He looked at the Investigator, who shrugged.

"Something's coming," said Williams quietly. "I can hear it. And whatever it is, this time it's not alone." He turned slowly round in a tight circle, and the colour gradually went out of his face. "They're all around us. Captain, I can hear things coming from every direction. All kinds of things."

"Be more specific," said Krystel. "What exactly are you hearing?"

"All kinds of things," said Williams. His voice began to rise. "They're getting closer. We've got to get out of here, while we still can. They're coming for us!"

"Take it easy," said Hunter. "Investigator, can you hear anything?"

"Nothing, Captain. But if his hearing is augmented . . ."

"Yeah," said Hunter.

Krystel drew her sword. "I think we should find some cover, Captain. We're too exposed out here."

"I think you're right, Investigator." Hunter drew his disrupter, and looked quickly about him. There were buildings all around, cloaked in shadows from the coming night, but none of them had obvious doorways. Over to his right, one of the buildings appeared to have been partially gutted by an explosion. Part of the street side had been torn away, leaving strands of metal like broken bones, and a jagged opening at the top of a small hill of rubble. Hunter started towards it, and the other two followed.

Climbing the rubble of broken stone and metal proved easy enough, and Hunter paused at the top to take out his field lantern and turn it on. The pale golden light showed a vast, empty room beyond the opening. The walls were covered with a silver metal tracery, forming disturbing patterns that bordered on the edge of meaning. Hunter looked back at the street below. He still couldn't see or hear anything, despite the extra height the hill of rubble gave him. He began to wonder if Williams hadn't been overreacting and jumping at his own shadow. And then the first whisper of sound came to him, from somewhere far off in the distance. He spun round, and glared in its general direction. Far off in the gloom, something was moving. Hunter crouched down behind one of the large outcroppings of rubble. Krystel had already found some cover. Williams had drawn his gun, but was still standing in plain view, staring off into the gathering dusk with his adjusted eyes.

"Oh, my God," he said faintly.

"What is it?" said Krystel. "What can you see?"

"Someone has opened the gates of Hell," said Williams. "And the damned are loose in the city."

Hunter shot a quick glance at Krystel, who just looked straight back at him. Hunter stared out into the dark, his breath steaming on the chill air. He felt even colder, now that they'd stopped moving. And then he caught his first glimpse of what was coming towards him, and a worse chill swept through him. A great tide of leaping, running, and crawling life came surging down the wide street, heading straight for the concealed Hell Squad; an endless flow of nightmares and monstrosities. There were things that walked on two legs and some that ran on four, and others that leaped through the air as though they were weightless. There were creatures with fangs and claws that snapped and tore at those around them. There were those who looked as though they'd somehow been horribly turned inside out, and some whose shapes made no sense at all.

Giant insects crawled along the sides of buildings like beetles on a coffin lid. Twisted shapes flapped through the air. The aliens screamed and roared and chattered, and there were sounds that might almost have been human cries or laughter. They came surging out of the darkness without end, driven by some unimaginable goad, drawing closer all the time. Hunter looked at the city's nightmares, and wanted to turn away and hide until they were gone. He couldn't bear the sight of them. Their foul shapes and insane structures were an offence against his reason.

But he couldn't just run away and hide. He was the Captain, and he had to set an example. Even if he was so scared he could hardly think straight, and the old familiar panic was gnawing at his nerves, threatening to break loose at any moment. His breathing was short and hurried, and he could feel sweat beading on his face. He looked down at his disrupter and saw that his hand was shaking. He swallowed hard and fought back the panic. It didn't matter that he was scared and couldn't cope. He had to cope. There was no one else. He took a long, shuddering breath, and felt some of the tension go out of him. There was a certain comfort in knowing that the worst that could happen had already happened. At least the waiting was over and there were no more surprises to worry about. He brought his disrupter to bear on the surging mass of aliens. His hand was still shaking, but so slightly now that only he would know it. He grabbed Williams with his free hand and pulled him back behind some cover. Williams jerked his arm free and glared at Hunter. Hunter glared right back at him. There were times when he wondered if the doctor was trying to get himself killed.

The aliens were fast approaching the hill of rubble, and for the first time Hunter was able to make out the true horror of their condition. None of them had a fixed form. Their shapes came and went like so many whims or fleeting memories, never the same two moments running. Flesh flowed on their bones like melting wax, sliding endlessly from one form to another. New eyes surfaced in the bubbling flesh, and new arms burst out of their heaving sides. Hunter was reminded briefly of the statues he'd seen on the open plain, depicting creatures made up of bits and pieces from various species, neither one thing nor another. Perhaps they had been meant as a warning after all.

"Stand ready," said Hunter. His voice sounded gratifyingly calm and even. "Dr. Williams, wait until they're close enough for you to pick a specific target before you use your disrupter. Investigator, you've had the most combat experience. You take the point, and the doctor and I will guard your sides."

"Understood, Captain." Krystel looked out over the milling horrors, and smiled unpleasantly. Hunter shivered. There was something horribly wild and eager about her smile. She might almost have been looking at an approaching lover.

"We can't stay here!" said Williams suddenly. "Look at them! They'll be here any minute, and there's nothing we can do to stop them. We've got to get out of here while we still can!"

He scrambled away from his section of cover and headed for the opening in the wall. Hunter grabbed him by the arm and pulled him back. "Don't be a fool, Williams!

How far would you get on your own? Stand fast, and guard the Investigator's side. Or I swear I'll cut you down myself."

Williams snarled at him, but remained where Hunter had put him. "We don't have to stay here! We could still fall back into the building and barricade the hole with the force screen."

"We've talked this through before, Doctor. The screen would only last as long as its energy crystals permitted, and then it would collapse. By which time the aliens would undoubtedly have us surrounded. We'll fall back into the building when we have to, and not before. Now activate your shield and stand ready. Company's coming."

Williams turned away in disgust, and slapped his left wrist against his side. The glowing force shield appeared on his arm, murmuring quietly to itself. Hunter looked at Krystel. Her shield was already up. She was still grinning at the approaching aliens. Hunter drew his Service dagger from his boot, hefted his gun once, and then activated his shield. The aliens were very near now. He moved forward a pace, so that he could guard the Investigator's left side while still being comfortably close to his chosen piece of cover. It wasn't much use as cover, if truth be told, but it would have to do. The Investigator stood in plain view of the aliens, looking strong and confident, as though cover was something only lesser mortals needed.

She's an Investigator, thought Hunter. *Maybe she doesn't need cover, at that.*

He looked out at the approaching aliens, and his heart missed a beat. They filled the street from side to side, for as far as he could see. There were monstrosities beyond counting, of every shape and size.

This isn't fair, thought Hunter bitterly. *We're not up to this. We're just a Hell Squad. A full company of shock troops would have their work cut out here. We're not fighters. Not really. We're just rejects and walking wounded; the outcasts and the expendables.*

He took a deep breath and let it go. *What the hell; maybe we'll get lucky.*

The aliens were close now, the nearest only yards away. There were things like giant crustaceans, with huge pincer claws and staring eyes on the end of stalks. Their many-jointed legs clattered loudly on the street. As Hunter watched, one of the crustaceans suddenly swelled in size. Its carapace began to bubble and melt, and a pair of membranous wings burst out of its back. It threw itself into the air, its wings stretching impossibly wide as it soared towards the Hell Squad. Hunter took careful aim with his disrupter and fired. The searing energy beam hit the creature squarely in the lower thorax, and it exploded, scattering shards of broken chitin like shrapnel. The body fell into the alien horde, and they tore it apart. The separate parts writhed and twisted even as they were consumed. Those aliens that couldn't reach the downed creature clawed and tore at each other. None of them died. They were beyond death now. The great device had seen to that.

Giant centipedes clattered along the street, hundreds of feet long, their small bulbous heads nothing more than mouth and teeth. Maggots writhed in their flesh. Williams blew one in half with his disrupter. The two halves became separate creatures and pressed forward, driven by the same unrelenting determination that possessed the rest of the horde. Hunter wondered briefly what that drive was. It couldn't be just hunger. Perhaps it was simply the Hell Squad's normality, their fixed shapes, that drew the aliens like moths to a bright burning flame. Hatred? Regret? Hunter shook his head. Those were human emotions.

The aliens came surging forward, and the Hell Squad met them with flashing steel. Multicoloured blood flew on the air as steel blades cut into shifting flesh, but still the aliens pressed forward. They could be hurt but not killed, and they were used to pain. Only their habit of turning on their own injured kept the monsters from overrunning the Squad.

Hunter swung his knife with grim efficiency, protecting himself and guarding the Investigator as best he could. The razor-sharp edges of the force shield helped. On Krystel's other side, Williams swung his sword as though it were weightless, and never missed his target. *More augmentations,* thought Hunter. *He must be crammed full of implants from head to toe.* He just hoped they were fully charged. Investigator Krystel was in her element. She swung her claymore double-handed, and the heavy blade sheared through the shifting flesh as though it was nothing more than mist or smoke. She was chanting something to the rhythm of her blows, in a harsh guttural language Hunter didn't recognise, and her face was alive with an awful happiness. He looked away and concentrated his fear and anger on the aliens. His knife wasn't doing much damage, but just the scent of spilled blood was often enough to send the surrounding creatures into a feeding frenzy.

Hunter stepped back a pace to avoid an alien's snapping mouth, and nearly fell as the rubble shifted suddenly underfoot. Regaining his balance with an effort, he used the flat of his shield to push the monster back. Its teeth clattered and broke on the energy field. Hunter tried to use the larger blocks of stone as cover, but his footing was too precarious now to allow for much movement. The alien tide broke ceaselessly against the foot of the hill, always pressing forward, no matter how many of them fell to the Squad's weapons or each other's hunger. And none of them died, no matter how badly they were hurt. Within the space of a few moments they rose unharmed from deadly wounds, and half-eaten bodies re-formed around shattered bones to fight again. Hunter felt a growing despair as he realised there was no way to win, no matter how well he fought. Sooner or later the undying aliens would drag him down, and if he was lucky, his death would be quick. He wondered briefly if he too would rise from the dead, to kill and be killed again and again, but his mind shied away from the horror of such a thought.

The rubble lurched again under his feet, and then suddenly broke apart, great cracks running jaggedly across the hill. From underneath the shifting stones and metal came the sound of something huge, burrowing towards the surface. Translucent tentacles burst up out of the cracks, searching blindly for prey. Williams cried out, as much in shock as fear, and cut desperately at the tentacles with his sword. Krystel ignored them, her wild smile unchanged as she fought back the alien horde with unflinching determination. Hunter wavered for a moment, uncertain what to do for the best, or even if there was anything he could do. The glistening tentacles were whipping back and forth, and it was clearly only a matter of moments before they caught one of the Squad. Hunter stepped back a pace, his heart hammering against his breastbone as he crouched down behind his shield, and then he stuck his gun into one of the cracks and pressed the stud. The brilliant beam of energy stabbed down into the bulk of what moved under the hill, and the rubble heaved underfoot like a wild swell at sea, as the dweller below howled in agony.

For a moment, everything seemed to stop as the horrid sound rose up out of the rubble, and then the tentacles snapped back into the cracks and were gone. The howl died away, and the horde pressed forward again. Krystel met them eagerly with her smile and her flashing sword. The keen steel edge sliced through reaching hands and tentacles, and punched through bones and cartilage like paper. A great crawling insect with bulbous eyes darted in under her reach, its razor-sharp mandibles snapping hungrily. Without slowing her attack, Krystel took her cigar out of her mouth and thrust the glowing end into one of the creature's protruding eyes. The eye burst and the huge insect scuttled backwards, shaking its head violently, as though it could throw off the pain. Other creatures fell on it, and it disappeared under a heaving mass of hands and teeth.

Hunter moved in close at Krystel's side again, but he knew he couldn't last much longer. His breathing was coming fast and uneven, and the cold air burned in his lungs. He was drenched in sweat despite the chill, and his back and arms ached from wielding the dagger and shield without rest. Krystel seemed as fresh as ever, but Hunter knew that even an Investigator's training had its limits. Williams was beginning to slow down too. They had to fall back soon or they'd be overrun. But falling back could give the aliens the opening they needed. *Damned if we do, damned if we don't,* thought Hunter sourly. *And a better definition of a Hell Squad I never heard.* More than that, there were creatures in the horde now that none of their weapons would be able to stop. There were glowing mists that hugged the ground, holding indistinct mouths that gnawed at the rubble. There were creatures of churning liquid that fell apart when their surface tension was broken, only to form and re-form endlessly. A sword or a gun could only do so much.

Williams glanced back over his shoulder. The hole in the wall was only a few feet away now, but it might as well have been a few miles. If he turned and ran, some monstrosity or another would be sure to drag him down. But he couldn't stay where he was. Only the speed and strength of his augmentations was keeping the aliens at bay, and the power in his energy crystals wasn't endless. No, if he was going to make a run for it, he needed a distraction, something to draw the aliens' attention away from him for the few seconds it would take him to reach the hole in the wall and safety. But what could distract the aliens? Perhaps only one thing; the one thing the aliens wanted so badly. A human death.

Williams' face went blank as the thought took hold. He needed Hunter and Krystel to protect him. And there was always the chance of his being found out. But in this confused press of bodies, who could blame him if a shot from his gun was to go tragically astray? No one would be able to prove anything; and surely it was better for one to die than all three. He glanced briefly at Krystel and Hunter. The Investigator's skills and expertise made her an invaluable member of the Squad. Captain Hunter, on the other hand, was nobody special—just an authoritative voice. He wouldn't be missed. Williams smiled slightly. It was all coming together. One shot in the back, and Hunter would go down. The aliens would fight over his body, and he and the Investigator could seize the moment to get away. Perfect. Williams kept the aliens at bay with his sword and shield, waited for just the right moment, and then aimed his disrupter at Hunter's back. He never saw the wide-winged creature that swept down towards him, claws extended.

The first Hunter knew of it was when he heard Williams scream. He glanced round, startled, and saw the winged thing struggling to lift Williams into the air. The alien had a long, leathery body and great membranous wings, but Williams was still writhing and struggling, despite the claws sunk deep into his body. The alien finally lurched into the air with its captive. Williams' blood fell across the horde of monstrosities, and they went mad at the taste and smell of it. They reached up for Williams, their arms and necks stretching impossibly. Krystel grabbed Hunter's arm and urged him towards the hole in the wall while the horde was distracted. He hesitated, but one look was enough to show him there was nothing he could do to save Williams. The winged thing had dropped too low under the doctor's weight, and the horde dragged it down and pulled Williams away from it. He was still struggling and screaming as the horde tore him apart.

Krystel was already running towards the hole in the wall. Hunter started after her, and then hesitated again as he saw something metal glinting on the ground. It was Williams' sword. Hunter thrust his dagger back into his boot, snatched up the sword, and ran after Krystel. They reached the opening and charged through it before most of the aliens even realised they were gone. Hunter and Krystel stopped just inside the hole and looked quickly about them.

They were in a huge empty room, lit only by the dim light falling through the jagged hole. Hunter and Krystel moved quickly to get out of the light, and set their backs against the wall on either side of the opening. Hunter's breathing finally began to slow a little. Outside, it sounded as though the horde was still diverted by Williams' death, but Hunter knew that wouldn't last long. He hefted Williams' sword. It had a fine balance, and it felt good to have a sword in his hand again. He hadn't realised how much he'd missed it until he had to make do with just his dagger. A disrupter and a force shield were powerful weapons, but in the end somehow it always came down to cold steel, and the man who used it. He looked across at Krystel. She was breathing hard and covered in sweat, but she still looked calmer and fresher than he did.

"What happened to Williams?" he said hoarsely.

Krystel shrugged. "He must have got careless. Or unlucky. It happens."

Hunter nodded tiredly. "All right, what do we do next?"

"You're the Captain."

Hunter looked at her resentfully, but knew she was right. For all her skills, he had the most experience, so the responsibility was his—even though all he really wanted was to sit right down where he was and hide, and hope the aliens would give up and go away. He was tired. He couldn't recall when he'd ever felt this tired. It was the strain, of course; the never-ending tension. . . .

"All right," he said finally, trying hard to at least sound confident. "We can't stay here. The aliens will be in here after us at any minute. Let's get moving. The sooner we put some distance between us and them, the better."

He moved steadily towards the other side of the room, wincing as his aching joints protested. The Investigator took the field lantern from her backpack and turned it on before following him. The soft golden light was lost in the darkness of the huge room, but it was enough for Hunter to make out an open doorway in the far wall. He broke into a run, and Krystel padded along beside him. They'd just reached the doorway when the light from behind them was suddenly cut off. Hunter glanced back to find that something huge, armoured, and headless had wedged itself into the hole in the wall. He raised his gun and pressed the stud. The beam of searing energy punched clean through the armoured body. The alien screamed hoarsely, but did not die. Hunter ran through the open doorway, with Krystel close behind.

They found themselves in a long, high-ceilinged hall filled with rows of squat alien machinery that disappeared into the darkness beyond the lantern light. Hunter and Krystel slowed to a halt. Lights gleamed on some of the machines, and there was a low, unpleasant hum on the air, shuddering in their bones. Krystel looked behind her.

"They're coming after us, Captain. I can hear them."

Hunter glared back the way they'd come. "We can't outrun them. We need to slow them down, buy us some time." He smiled suddenly, and pulled one of the concussion grenades from his bandolier. He primed it, and then rolled it along the ground so that it stopped just inside the doorway. "All right, Investigator; let's get the hell out of here."

They ran between the alien machinery, surrounded by a halo of light from the field lantern. It seemed to Hunter that they ran for a long time, but still the hall stretched away before them, and the grenade didn't go off. And then the floor shook under their feet, and a blast of roaring air sent them flying forward. The explosion was deafeningly loud in the confined space, and slivers of stone and metal flew through the air like shrapnel. Hunter and Krystel raised their force shields above their heads to protect themselves and crouched down to present a smaller target. After a while, they looked back. The hall was blocked with rubble from the shattered walls. Hunter and Krystel shared a grin, then ran on into the darkness.

They reached the end of the hall, but there was no doorway. Krystel raised her gun and blew a hole through the wall. They clambered through the sharp-edged opening and found themselves in a long, featureless corridor. Glowing rods were set into the ceiling at irregular intervals. Krystel strapped the field lantern to her belt so as to leave one hand free, then stopped and looked quickly back through the hole. Hunter heard it too. The aliens had broken through into the hall of machines and were coming after them. Hunter and Krystel ran down the corridor at full pelt. Hunter had no idea where he was going, but anything was better than waiting around for the aliens to catch up with them.

The corridor seemed to go on forever, with never a doorway or opening anywhere. The first sounds of pursuit began to echo behind them, together with an occasional inhuman roar. Hunter didn't look back. He didn't want to know how close the aliens were. Krystel pulled a grenade from her bandolier and held it in her hand, ready for use. They finally rounded a corner and plunged through an opening into the base of a tower. The familiar ramp wound up the inside wall. Krystel looked at it dubiously.

"If we let ourselves be chased up there, eventually we're going to run out of ramp. And the top of a high tower is a hell of a place to be cornered."

"I couldn't agree more," said Hunter. "But we're not going that far. How close are the aliens?"

Krystel looked back down the corridor. "Too close, and getting closer."

"Figures. Have you still got your grenade? Good. Use it to slow the bastards down a bit, and then follow me up the ramp."

Hunter started up the ramp as Krystel turned to face the corridor. She primed the grenade and rolled it down the corridor into the darkness. In the distance, something that glowed with an eerie violet light hissed like a fire hose. Krystel snarled silently in return, and then hurried up the ramp after Hunter. She found him waiting for her in a doorway leading off the ramp onto the next floor. The grenade blew, and the ramp trembled under their feet. A chorus of inhuman screams and howls echoed up from the corridor below. Hunter and Krystel shared a smile, and then Hunter led the Investigator through the doorway into a dark, empty room.

They hurried across the room and through an open doorway into another room. Metallic streamers hung from the ceiling, twisting and turning slowly, though no breeze stirred the air. Hunter and Krystel crossed the room as quickly as they dared, threading their way through the streamers while being very careful not to touch them. The streamers looked harmless enough, but both the Captain and the Investigator had learned to distrust everything they found in the city; particularly things that moved when they shouldn't. The next room was empty, and a dead end. Hunter stopped and listened, but everything seemed quiet. He nodded briefly to the Investigator.

"Stay in the doorway. Keep an eye open for uninvited guests."

Krystel unstrapped her field lantern and put it down, then moved away to stand guard in the doorway, sword and force shield at the ready. Hunter aimed his disrupter at the middle of the floor and pressed the stud. The energy bolt blasted a wide hole through the floor. Cracks spread out from the hole, and Hunter watched anxiously for a long moment before the floor finally settled again. He holstered his gun, picked up the lantern, knelt down, and lowered it through the hole. The room below held a number of steel and crystal shapes that might have been machines or sculptures, but was otherwise empty. Hunter studied the drop dubiously, and tried to tell himself it wasn't as far as it looked.

"Krystel! Any sign of the aliens?"

"Nothing yet, Captain."

"Then get over here. We're going back down a floor the hard way. With a little luck, that should throw the aliens off our trail long enough for us to make a discreet exit. I'll go first."

He put the lantern on the floor beside him, turned off his force shield, and sheathed his sword. He sat down on the edge of the hole and lowered his legs into it. With the light gone, he couldn't see how far the drop was. He wasn't sure whether that made him feel less or more nervous. In the end, he just gritted his teeth, and pushed himself off. He dropped for an unnervingly long moment, and then the floor slammed up against his feet. He fell in a sprawling heap and knocked the wind out of himself. He'd just about managed to get to his feet again when Krystel landed lightly beside him, lantern in hand.

"Are you all right, Captain?"

"Fine," he said quickly. "Just fine."

The room led out into a corridor. There were lighting rods set into the ceiling, but only a few of them were working. The corridor held only shadows, and there was no trace to show the aliens had ever been there. Hunter and Krystel crept quietly through the gloom, weapons at the ready, and soon passed into another corridor. They made their way cautiously across the ground floor of the building, jumping at every sound or moving shadow, until finally they found a doorway that led out onto the street.

Hunter gestured to Krystel to turn off the field lantern, and peered warily out the doorway into the gloom. The street was empty, and there was no sign of the aliens. Hunter stepped out onto the street, looked around, and then nodded for Krystel to join him. She did so, strapping the lantern to her belt just in case she needed it again in a hurry. The sun had dropped almost out of sight, and the sky was darkening towards night. Some distance away, the copper tower stood tall and enigmatic above the surrounding buildings.

Hunter turned to Krystel to tell her it was safe to move off, and then froze as the wall behind her cracked open and fell apart. Long branches of spiked vine burst out of the stonework, reaching for the Investigator. She threw herself to the ground and rolled out of reach, but by the time she was back on her feet again the vines had spilled out onto the street, forming an impenetrable barrier between her and the Captain. A score of leaping, hopping insects, each a foot long or more, came flying out of the wall and descended on Krystel, their long jaws snapping hungrily. She activated her force shield and met them with her sword. Hunter picked off one of the insects with his gun, exploding its dark grey carapace, but couldn't do anything else to help her. He threw himself at the twisting vines, hacking at them with his sword. The barbs rattled harmlessly against his steelmesh tunic and broke themselves against his force shield.

Krystel swung her sword double-handed, her cold grin back again. The huge insects fell beneath her blade, and the uninjured feasted on the fallen. Krystel laughed aloud. This was what she had been trained for, the moment that gave purpose to her life; to be the perfect, invincible killing machine. The aliens came to her and she slaughtered them, and was content.

Hunter finally used his next to the last grenade on the vines. The blast blew him a hole through the writing branches, and he forced his way through, ignoring the scratches to his bare face and hands. The Investigator had surrounded herself with crippled insects, and for the moment seemed to have run out of targets. He grabbed her arm and hustled her off down the street. For a moment she struggled against him, and then the killing fever left her, and she ran along beside him, heading for the copper tower.

And behind them came the aliens, in all their many shapes.

Corbie lifted his gun and fired blindly into the darkness. The brilliant energy bolt illuminated the hall of memories briefly, and punched a hole clean through the chest of the armoured alien as it tried to break through the wall. It screamed once as the darkness returned, a curiously high-pitched sound from such a large creature. Corbie glared wildly about him, and reached blindly for the esper. He knew she was somewhere close at hand—he could hear her dry heaving—but he couldn't seem to locate her with his hands. And then his fingers brushed against something hard and unyielding, and his heart missed a beat.

"Stand still," said Lindholm quickly. "And keep your hands to yourself. Start thrashing around in the dark and we'll end up killing each other. Turn on your force shield; that'll give us some light while I get the field lantern out of your backpack."

Corbie activated his shield, and the glowing energy field appeared on his arm, the pale light dispelling some of the darkness. Lindholm glanced briefly at the armoured alien lying slumped in the wreckage of the wall, and rummaged in Corbie's backpack for his lantern. Corbie grabbed DeChance by the shoulders and got her on her feet again. She leaned tiredly against him and clung to his arm for support. The dry heaves died away, leaving her pale and trembling. Corbie looked at her anxiously. Her face was gaunt and pinched, and her eyes didn't track. Off in the distance, from every side, there came the sound of alien screams and cries. They were getting closer. Lindholm finally got the lantern working, and the hall of memories reappeared around them.

"We've got to get out of here, Sven," said Corbie. "The esper's out of it, and the aliens will be here any minute."

"I think you're probably right," said Lindholm. He looked around for an exit, but there was only the doorway they'd come through. Part of one wall had collapsed, but the armoured alien blocked the way with its body, and already the creature was showing signs of stirring. Lindholm swore briefly, and pointed his disrupter at the floor. He pressed the stud, and the searing beam of energy smashed open a hole. The floor groaned and shuddered. Cracks spread out from the hole, but after a few moments the floor grew steady again. Corbie gave Lindholm a hard look.

"Down there? Are you kidding? There could be anything down there!"

"Have you got a better idea?"

Corbie scowled unhappily. "Some days you just shouldn't get out of bed in the morning."

Lindholm sat down on the floor and swung his legs into the hole. "I'll go first, and you can hand the esper down to me. Right?"

"Got it," said Corbie. He manhandled the unresisting esper over to the hole, and then waited impatiently as Lindholm lowered himself into the darkness. Corbie glared back through the open doorway. He couldn't see anything in the gloom, but he could hear the aliens drawing nearer. It sounded like there were a lot of them. Over in the wreckage of the wall, the armoured alien slowly raised its head. Its eyes glowed blue in the dim light. Corbie looked at the dazed esper, and wondered what the hell the memory sphere had shown her to produce such a violent reaction. On second thought, he decided he probably didn't want to know. Lindholm hissed at him from down in the hole, and Corbie carefully lowered the esper into Lindholm's waiting arms. DeChance murmured something indistinct, but didn't come out of her daze. The armoured alien heaved itself out of the wreckage of the broken wall. Corbie quickly sat down by the hole, and pushed himself off into the darkness below.

Under the floor he found himself in a circular tunnel some seven feet high. After the huge scale of the other buildings, the tunnel felt decidedly claustrophobic. Moisture ran down the rough stone walls and pooled on the floor. It smelled awful. Lindholm held up his lantern and looked up and down the tunnel. It stretched away into the distance for as far as he could see. Lindholm and Corbie looked at each other.

"So, which way now?" said Corbie.

"Beats me," said Lindholm. "One way is as good as another, I suppose."

"No," said DeChance. "That way."

She pointed down the tunnel with a trembling hand. Lindholm tentatively released his hold on her, and smiled encouragingly when she managed to stay upright without his support. Her eyes had focused again, but she looked awful. Her face was pale and haggard, the skin stretched tightly over the bones. Sweat ran down her face, and her eyes had a sunken, bruised look. Her hands were trembling violently.

"How are you feeling?" said Corbie gently.

DeChance grinned. "I'll live."

"What did the ball show you?" asked Lindholm.

"Not now," said DeChance. She pointed down the tunnel again. "We have to go that way, and quickly. The aliens will be here soon. They want us badly, and they won't give up. They want what makes us sane. Our certainty. I think this tunnel is part of what used to be the sewers. We'll follow the tunnel until we're somewhere near the copper tower, and then blast our way back out again."

"How are we going to know when we've reached the tower?" said Corbie.

"I'll know," said DeChance. "The device burns very brightly in my mind."

Corbie looked at Lindholm, who shrugged. Corbie shook his head disgustedly. "I might have known I'd end up having to make all the decisions in this group."

"But you do it so well, Russ," said Lindholm solemnly. "Haven't I always said you were natural officer material?"

"You know, Sven, you could be replaced."

"What by?"

"Practically anything."

A long, hooked leg bristling with thorns groped down through the hole from above. The Squad backed quickly away from it.

"Right," said Corbie. "That does it. Let's get moving. Sven, you've got the light so you take the lead. We'll follow. And let's not hang about, people. This strikes me as a very unlucky place to be cornered in."

He cut the probing leg in two with his sword. The severed end fell to lie twitching on the tunnel floor. Lindholm moved quickly off down the tunnel, and Corbie and DeChance hurried after him. Corbie took the esper's hand to guide her, and then had to fight to keep from snatching his hand back again. Her skin felt wet and slippery, and somehow . . . loose, as though she'd lost a lot of weight in a hurry. He started to say something, but DeChance began to tell him what she'd learned from the memory sphere, and he forgot his question as he listened. The intricate tale of broken dreams and raging madness took a long time to tell, and sounded all the worse for being told in such dark and claustrophobic conditions. By the time the esper had finished, both Corbie and Lindholm had taken to glancing anxiously over their shoulders at the darkness beyond the lantern light.

The tunnel began to slope noticeably downwards and the floor was covered in steadily deepening water. By the time DeChance stopped speaking, it was lapping up around their ankles. The water was dark and scummy, and there were things floating in it that Corbie preferred not to look at too closely. The esper and the marines waded along in silence for a while. The sound of their boots splashing through the water seemed unnaturally loud on the quiet.

"You think the great device is housed somewhere in the copper tower?" said Corbie finally.

"I think the tower *is* the device," said DeChance. "A single huge machine, still functioning after God knows how many centuries."

"So what are we going to do when we get there?" asked Corbie. "Blow it up?"

"I don't know. Maybe." DeChance rubbed at her forehead, as though bothered by a headache. "Somehow I don't think it'll be that simple. The device can defend itself against attacks if it has to." She broke off suddenly and stopped dead in her tracks. The two marines stopped with her. DeChance stared ahead into the darkness. "There's something there, something . . . strange. It's waiting for us to come to it."

Corbie and Lindholm trained their guns on the darkness. For a long moment, nobody moved. The Squad's force shields hummed loudly on the quiet. Corbie listened hard, but couldn't hear anything moving. The filthy water was calm and undisturbed.

"How close is it?" he whispered to DeChance.

The esper frowned. "It's waiting, just beyond the light. It feels . . . strange, unfinished."

"Maybe we should just turn around and go back," suggested Corbie.

"No!" DeChance urgently. "We have to get to the copper tower! It's our only hope. Besides, the creature would only follow us."

"Terrific," said Corbie. "This just gets better and better."

"We could always throw a grenade at it," said Lindholm.

Corbie looked at him. "In a confined space like this? Are you crazy? The blast would come straight back and make mincemeat out of us!"

"Sorry," said Lindholm. "I wasn't thinking."

"You'd better start quickly," said DeChance. "It's moving towards us."

Lindholm and Corbie levelled their guns on the darkness. DeChance drew hers, but her hand was still too unsteady to aim it. She activated her force shield and peered watchfully over the top of it. A faint, glowing light appeared deep in the dark of the tunnel, growing steadily stronger as it approached the Squad. Corbie bit back a curse as the creature's form became clear, lit by its own eerie light. It had no shape as such, only a frothing mass of eyes and bubbles that filled the tunnel from wall to wall like a wave of onrushing foam. Great snapping mouths appeared and disappeared as the creature surged forward. Lindholm fired his disrupter. The blast went right through the boiling mass. A few bubbles popped, but otherwise the beam had no effect. Corbie stepped forward and cut at the mass with his sword. The blade swept through the foam without pausing.

Corbie stumbled forward and fell on one knee, caught off balance by the lack of resistance. A snapping mouth tried for his hand and only just missed. More mouths reached for him. And then the creature came into contact with Corbie's shield, and the bubbles popped loudly on meeting the energy field. The fanged mouths disappeared back into the staring, boiling mass. Corbie swept his shield at it, and more bubbles burst. The creature began to quickly withdraw down the tunnel. In a few moments it had disappeared back into the darkness and was gone. Corbie got to his feet again, and shook his wet leg disgustedly.

"I just know I'm going to catch something horrible from this stuff. Esper, is that thing out there, waiting in the darkness, or is it still running?"

"Still running," said DeChance. "I don't think anything's been able to hurt it in a long time. Now let's get moving again, please. It's a long way to the copper tower, and we want to get there before dark. Things are worse in the city at night."

The Squad moved on through the narrow tunnel in their own little pool of light. The tunnel branched repeatedly, but the esper always seemed to know which way to go. Ceramic pipes lined the walls for long stretches, coiled around each other as often as not, before disappearing back into the stonework. *I suppose even an alien city needs good sewers,* thought Corbie. *And this place smells so bad it's got to be part of a sewer. I've known slaughterhouses that smelled better than this.*

The water grew deeper, lapping up around their knees. Fungi began to appear on the walls in shades of grey and white, often spread in wide patches more than two inches thick. Corbie was careful not to touch any of it. It looked like it might be hungry. Patches of swirling scum appeared on the surface of the water, and Corbie watched them suspiciously. He had a strong feeling some of them were following him. And then the Squad came to a sudden halt as they spotted a large smooth-edged hole in the stone wall to their right, some distance ahead.

"Can you sense anything, esper?" asked Corbie quietly.

"I'm not sure. There's something there, but it's shielded. I can't get a hold on it." She rubbed tiredly at her forehead. "It could be some creature's lair, or even some form of machinery."

"You stay here," said Corbie. "Sven and I will go take a look at it."

"You could have at least asked for volunteers," said Lindholm mildly. "Power's gone to your head, Russ."

"Moan, moan, moan," said Corbie. "You never want to do anything fun."

The two marines moved slowly forward, gun and sword at the ready. Their force shields muttered quietly to themselves. The hole in the wall seemed to grow larger the closer the marines got. Finally, they stood before a six foot wide hole, studying the darkness within from behind the safety of their force shields.

"Can't see a damned thing," muttered Corbie. "How about you, Sven?"

"Nothing. Can't hear anything either. I suppose it could be a lair that was abandoned some time back. The esper said the aliens had all been asleep for a long time."

"True. And I can't imagine anything alien enough to stay down here by choice."

Deep within the hole, something moved. Lindholm and Corbie raised their guns reflexively, only to freeze in place as an endless tide of darkness came rushing out over them. The esper cried out once, but neither of them heard her.

Corbie was standing on a snow-swept battlefield, surrounded by the dead. There was blood on his uniform, only some of it his. The double moons of the Hyades drifted on the night skies. The Ghost Warriors had been and gone, and the Empire marines had fallen before them. The marines were first-class soldiers, but they were only flesh and blood, and they'd stood no chance against the Legions of the living dead. Blood stained the snow all around, and the bodies of the slain stretched for as far as Corbie could see. Nothing moved save a single tattered banner flapping in the wind. Corbie's sword was broken and his gun was exhausted. Out of a whole Company of Imperial marines, he was the only survivor.

Ghost Warriors. Dead bodies controlled by computer implants. The ultimate terror troops; unthinking, unfeeling, unstoppable. Corbie had thought himself a brave man, until he'd had to face the Ghost Warriors. They tested his courage again and again, until finally they broke it. The Legions of the dead were enough to break anyone.

Corbie looked around the silent battlefield. It seemed to him that he should be somewhere else, but he couldn't think where that might be. There was a sudden movement close at hand, and Corbie fell back a step as one of the Empire corpses lifted its head from the snow and looked at him. Dried blood had turned half its face into a dark crimson mask, but its eyes gleamed brightly. It rose unsteadily to its feet to stand before Corbie. There was a gaping wound in its chest where one of the Ghost Warriors had ripped its heart out. The corpse grinned suddenly, revealing bloody teeth.

"You always were a survivor, Corbie."

"Major . . ." Corbie tried to explain, to apologise, but his voice was harsh and dry, and the words wouldn't come.

"Don't talk to me, survivor. You haven't the right. We stood our ground, followed our orders, and fought and died, as marines should. You chose not to, survivor."

"I stood my ground."

"Only until it became clear that we were losing. Until it was clear the Company hadn't a hope in hell against the Legions. We stood and fought to the last man. You burrowed in among the bodies of the fallen, smeared yourself with blood, and hoped you'd be mistaken for just another corpse. And so the Company fell, and you alone survived to tell of it. I had such hopes for you, Corbie. But you betrayed us. You should have died with us, where you belonged."

"Someone had to survive, to warn Command."

"That wasn't why you did it. You were afraid. You've been afraid ever since." The corpse drew its sword. "Well, solider, now's your chance to pay in full."

Corbie threw away his broken sword, and drew the long Service dagger from his boot. "Only a fool dies for no good reason."

Their blades met, the clash of steel on steel carrying clearly across the silent battlefield.

Lindholm stood in the centre of the Great Arena, and all around him the Golgotha crowds cheered their appreciation of another death. The losing gladiator was dragged away, leaving a bloody trail behind him. It wasn't a subtle crowd gathered here today. They had no eye for the finer points of swordsmanship and defence. They wanted blood and suffering, and they didn't care whose. They'd paid to see death, right there in front of them, and they couldn't get enough of it. Their cheers grew louder and more frenzied as Lindholm's next opponent entered the Arena. Even before he turned to look, Lindholm knew who it was; who it would have to be. Tall, lithe, and graceful, Elena Dante acknowledged the cheers of the crowd, and saluted Lindholm with her sword. Dante, the smiling killer, the darling of the Golgotha crowds.

"I never wanted to fight you, Elena," said Lindholm quietly.

"It was bound to happen sooner or later, Sven," said Dante. "That's how the Arena works. Don't think I'll go easy on you, just because we're friends."

"More than friends."

"Maybe. It still doesn't make any difference. Out here on the sands there are only winners and losers. And I always fight to win."

"You can't kill me," said Lindholm. "Not after all we've meant to each other."

"You always were a romantic, Sven." Dante grinned widely. "Tell you what. We both know I'm going to win, so you just put up a good fight, give the crowd their thrills, and I promise you a quick death."

"You'd do that for me?" said Lindholm.

"Sure. What are friends for?"

Lindholm frowned. "I remember this. I've been here before. We fought in the Arena, and I killed you."

"That's right, Sven. And then you killed the fixer who arranged the match, and twenty-seven other Arena officials, before they finally dragged you down, clapped the irons on you, and gave you to the Hell Squads. But now I'm back, and you're going to have to kill me all over again. If you can."

Their swords met in a clash of steel.

DeChance stood knee-deep in filthy water in a tunnel beneath the alien city, and stared passionlessly at the familiar figure emerging from the hole in the wall. Corbie and Lindholm stood unmoving between her and the hole, staring blindly into the gloom. The familiar figure stepped into the lantern light. He was of average height and weight, with the quiet bland looks that can make a man invisible in a crowd. He smiled confidently at DeChance.

"Hello, Meg. Surprised to see me?"

"You're not real," said DeChance flatly. "There's no way you could be here, on Wolf IV. You're still out there in the Empire somewhere, doing what you do best. Getting people to trust them, and then betraying them for a handful of change."

He laughed quietly. "I'm as real as you want me to be, Meg. Believe in me and I'm here, as accurate as your memories can make me. And you do want to see me again, don't you? Even after everything that happened, there's a part of you that never stopped caring for me;

never stopped believing that deep down I cared for you."
He smiled warmly at her. "After all, what did I do that was
so bad? We all have to make a living."

DeChance moved a step closer to him. "I loved you.
Trusted you. Gave you every credit I had, to get me a
berth on a ship heading for Mistworld. I would have been
safe there; finally free from the Empire and the way it's
always treated espers. You were going to join me there,
and we were going to make a life together. But there was
no berth and there was no ship, and when the Security
Guards came for me you were nowhere to be seen. I found
out about you later, of course. But by then I'd already been
condemned to the Hell Squads."

"Of course," said the smiling figure. "They always find
out when it's too late. I do try to be professional in my
work. Francis Shrike; licensed traitor, double-dealing a
speciality." He cocked his head to one side, and fixed
her with a glittering eye. "You're still not sure how you
feel about me, are you? Are you angry at me for betraying
you, or at yourself, for trusting me? Could you really have
been so blind and foolish as to love someone who didn't
give a damn about you?"

"I know who was to blame." DeChance's sword seemed
almost to leap into her hand. "I know who I hate."

Shrike shook his head condescendingly. "You always did
carry a grudge, Meg. But things can be different here. I can
be anything you want me to be. I can love you like you've
always wanted to be loved. I can be everything you ever
dreamed of. Just put down your sword and come to me."

DeChance moved forward a step, and then stopped.
"Francis . . ."

"Come to me, Meg. I'm all yours."

DeChance lifted her sword and gripped the blade tightly
with her left hand. Blood ran down the blade as the keen
edges cut into her flesh. The pain ran through her like a
shock of cold water, and she grinned tightly at the figure
before her.

"Nice try, but you're not Francis. You're not even real.
And I hate him too much to be satisfied with a cheap

imitation." She tore her gaze away with an effort, and looked at the two marines, still standing silent and motionless. "What are they seeing? What faces are you showing them?"

"Whatever they want to see. It doesn't matter. They'll be mine soon."

"That's what you think," said DeChance. She sheathed her sword, drew her disrupter, and shot him at point-blank range. The brilliant beam of energy tore through his gut. Shrike's mouth stretched impossibly wide as he screamed. Corbie and Lindholm awoke with a start and looked about in confusion, torn abruptly from their dreams.

"It was just a trick," said DeChance quickly. "Whatever you saw, it wasn't real. It seems we've come across an alien with very strong esp. It tried to kill us with our own fears and desires."

DeChance and the marines glared at the creature before them. Under the pressure of their minds, the alien's shape began to blur and change, its features rising and falling as it tried to be three people at once. It quickly lost control, its humanity falling away like a discarded coat. The features fell apart, the eyes sliding down the face and sinking into the skin. The mouth widened and sprouted jagged teeth. The hands grew claws, and its back humped. What had appeared to be clothes became armoured scales, and a row of spikes burst out of its back. Corbie and Lindholm trained their guns on the creature and quickly backed away.

"Forget the guns," said DeChance. "I already tried that. There's a better way."

She concentrated, focusing all her esp into a single burst of hate and rage, and threw it at the creature. The alien shrank back, snarled once, and then turned and disappeared down the tunnel and into the darkness. They could hear it running for a while, and then even that faded away to nothing.

DeChance leaned back against the tunnel wall, her eyes hot and moist. Corbie looked at her with concern. She hadn't looked well for some time, but there was no denying she looked worse now. Her face was horribly pale and dripping with sweat. Her eyes were sunk deep into her face, and her whole body seemed to be trembling. Corbie started to reach out a hand to her, but withdrew it when DeChance glared at him.

"I'm fine. Just let me be."

"Why haven't the aliens used esp against us before?" asked Lindholm.

"I don't know," said DeChance. "I suppose esp varies as much in them as it does among humans. The sphere showed me what happened when they use it on each other, but it would take an extremely strong projective telepath to work on non-telepaths like you. Or perhaps the aliens are simply growing more powerful as the great device awakens. It's getting stronger all the time. It has been ever since . . ."

"You awakened it," said Lindholm.

"Oh yes," said DeChance bitterly. "I was the one who woke it up. I'm to blame. I'm to blame for everything that's happened here." Her voice began to rise sharply. "If I hadn't been a part of the Hell Squad, none of this would have happened. The device would have slept on undisturbed if it hadn't been for me, and you'd all have been perfectly safe!"

"Take it easy," said Corbie soothingly. "No one's blaming you for anything. Right, Sven? If you hadn't triggered the device, some colonist with esp would have, and who knows how large a colony would have been endangered then?"

DeChance said nothing. For a long moment the three of them just stood together in their little pool of light, looking out at the darkness.

"Is this likely to happen again?" said Corbie finally. "If the aliens can tap into our minds, there's no telling what we might end up facing. All our nightmares, every bad dream we ever had, could be out there somewhere, just waiting for a chance to get at us. And I don't know about you two, but I've had some pretty awful dreams in my time."

DeChance smiled crookedly. "Most of the aliens aren't that powerful, even with the device to back them up. What we're seeing are the aliens' nightmares, given shape and form."

"How much further is it to the copper tower?" asked Lindholm.

"Not far," said DeChance. "The tunnel should start sloping upwards soon, and then we can start thinking about getting out of here."

"Can't be too soon for me," said Corbie. "My skin's starting to pucker from the smell."

They moved on into the darkness, splashing through the foul water. From time to time Corbie thought he saw things swimming in the water, things the size of his fist that seemed to be mostly teeth and eyes. Corbie said nothing to the others. As long as the things in the water kept their distance, he was happy to live and let live, and he didn't want to upset the esper. The tunnel slanted sharply upwards, and Corbie allowed himself to think hopeful thoughts about breathing fresh air again. And then the esper stopped suddenly, and the marines stopped with her. Corbie's heart sank. Every time DeChance stopped like that it meant something really unpleasant was about to happen. The esper stared into the darkness ahead, frowning unhappily.

"There's something ahead, isn't there?" said Lindholm.

The esper nodded. "It's big. Very big."

"It can't be that big," objected Corbie. "The tunnel's only seven feet high."

"It's very big and very powerful," said the esper, as though she hadn't heard him. "I don't think our weapons are going to be enough this time."

"Great," said Corbie. "Just great. What are we going to do now, turn round and run back the way we've come?"

A great roar sounded out of the darkness, deafeningly loud, echoing and re-echoing from the stonework. Corbie levelled his disrupter at the tunnel ahead, and then fell back a step involuntarily as a gust of wind hit him in the face. Lindholm and the esper fell back with him as the alien appeared in the lantern light. It filled the tunnel completely, a huge mound of leathery flesh, with a ring of unblinking eyes surrounding a drooling maw.

"It's like some monstrous worm," whispered DeChance. "It's dozens of feet long. I can't sense the end of it."

The maw widened suddenly, growing and growing until the alien seemed nothing but a huge mouth, filling the tunnel from wall to wall. There was a smell of rotting meat as the creature exhaled. Corbie had a sudden vision of the three of them running down the tunnel, chased by a ravening maw that left no room for escape. He aimed his gun into the mouth. DeChance suddenly grabbed his arm.

"No! Aim for the ceiling! We're only a few feet from the surface. Blast us a way out of here and bring the tunnel down between us and the alien!"

Corbie fired unhesitatingly at the ceiling. The energy beam smashed through the thick stonework, and daylight fell into the tunnel as part of the ceiling collapsed. Debris rained down around the Squad, and they had to shelter under their force shields until it stopped. The alien roared again, and pressed forward another yard, scooping up the broken stone into its drooling maw. Lindholm fired his gun into the creature's mouth. It roared deafeningly, and lurched forward another few feet.

"Forget it!" snapped DeChance, turning off her force shield. "We have to get out of here while we can."

Lindholm nodded quickly. He put away his gun, turned off his shield, and made a stirrup with his hands. DeChance put her foot into it, and the marine boosted her up into the hole in the ceiling. The esper found a handhold, and pulled herself up and out onto the street above. Corbie turned off his force shield and followed her out the same way. The alien surged forward, crushing the stones on the floor under its immense bulk. Lindholm calmly pulled a concussion grenade from his bandolier, primed it, and tossed it into the gaping mouth, which snapped shut reflexively. Lindholm pushed some of the larger pieces of rubble together, climbed up onto them and pulled himself up into the hole. Corbie and DeChance hauled him out onto the street.

He rolled quickly away from the opening, and seconds later there was a muffled roar from below as the grenade went off. Blood and gore fountained up out of the hole, and cracks spread across the street.

"Nice one, Sven," said Corbie.

The three of them got to their feet and looked around them. The sun had sunk almost out of sight, and the green sky was darkening towards night. The city had become little more than shapes and shadows, with the occasional lighted window. The copper tower loomed above its surrounding buildings, less than half a mile away. Corbie shivered, and checked that his heating elements were set at maximum.

"Still no sign of the rest of the Squad," said Lindholm. "I hope they're having an easier time than us."

Corbie sniffed. "They probably had an attack of common sense and got the hell out of here."

"We'd better keep moving," said DeChance. "There are aliens nearby. More than I can count. They know we're here, and they're closing in on us."

She ran down the street without stopping to see if the marines were following. They looked quickly at each other, shared a sour smile, and hurried after her. From close at hand came the screams and cries of pursuing aliens, as the first of the unsteady creatures spilled onto the street after the fleeing Squad.

And in the copper tower, the great device waited patiently for them to come to it.

CHAPTER SEVEN

The Sleep of Reason

MONSTERS roamed the city streets. Some flew in the air, while others burrowed in the earth. Creatures formed by madness and obsession made their way to the copper tower, summoned by a voice they could not refuse. They no longer remembered why, but the echo of that voice moved within them, whatever shape they wore, and always would. The sun had fallen, and darkness lay across the city. Strange lights burned in the silent buildings as more and more creatures awoke from their centuries-long sleep and went out into the streets. Hideous shapes crept and crawled between structures they no longer recognised, in a city they had long since forgotten. They had lived for centuries, and might live for centuries more, but they did not know it. The awful thing they had done to themselves had trapped them forever in the here and now; in a single endless moment of existence. They had forgotten what they were, and what they had hoped to be. Only the great device remembered. And it was insane.

Hunter and Krystel ran down a twisting street, between stone monoliths with blazing windows and looming edifices of steel and crystal. The darkness hung around them like a listening stranger, and from every intersection they passed came more shapes and monstrosities to join the boiling pack that pursued them. Hunter was fighting for air, and his back and leg muscles screamed for rest, but he didn't dare slow his pace. The aliens were close on their heels, and drawing closer. The darkness hid most of the shapes that followed them, for which Hunter was grateful.

A shining figure stepped out of a stone monolith and reached for Krystel with phosphorescent hands. She cut sideways with her sword without slowing her pace, and severed the nearest hand. It fell sparking and sputtering into the street, and the creature howled wordlessly. Hunter thought briefly about using his disrupter, but decided against it as the alien fell back, clutching at its ruined arm with its remaining hand. The disrupter's energy crystals were running low, and he only used the gun now when there was no other choice.

He ran on after Krystel, hurdling the twitching hand in the street without slowing. His breath burned in his lungs, and sweat ran down his heaving sides. He glared at the Investigator. She'd been running and fighting just as much as him, and she wasn't even breathing hard. She was even smiling slightly as she shook the last creature's shimmering blood from her sword. Hunter shook his head wearily and blinked away the sweat that ran down into his eyes. It seemed some of the things he'd heard about Investigators and their training weren't exaggerations after all.

A winged shape dropped out of the sky towards Hunter, its wings flapping loosely as its yard-long beak stabbed down at his face. He raised his force shield above his head, and the beak shattered on the energy field. The alien screamed and flapped away, blood dripping from its ruined face. A barbed tentacle shot up out of the pursuing pack and pulled the alien down. The pack fell on it and tore it apart. Hunter and Krystel ran on.

The copper tower stood tall and imposing against the skyline; an enigmatic silhouette against the alien night. Hunter scowled at it. He'd chosen the tower as a rendezvous point because it could be clearly seen from anywhere in the city, but he was beginning to wish he'd chosen somewhere closer. He'd lost track of how long he'd been running, but the tower seemed as far away as ever. Something moved in a nearby alleyway, and the Investigator turned her gun on it.

"No, Krystel!" Hunter knocked her arm aside at the last moment. "They're friends."

Krystel lowered her gun as Megan DeChance and the two marines plunged out of the alleyway to run alongside them. They all managed a quick nod of greeting to each other, but none of them had the breath for conversation. They ran on, with Krystel and the esper leading the way. Hunter looked at the two marines, and winced. Their uniforms were torn and stained with blood. Fatigue had put bruises under their eyes, and made their movements heavy and plodding. They didn't look like they could run much further. Hunter smiled sourly. He didn't suppose he looked much better.

But he and the rest of the Squad would run as far as they had to; because the only alternative was to lie down and die. Hunter looked at the esper's back and frowned. He'd only caught a brief glimpse of DeChance's face, but she'd looked to be in an even worse state than the marines. If there was a weak link in the Squad, she was it. And valuable as she was, Hunter hoped she wouldn't fall. None of them had the strength left to carry her. The esper began to speak, and Hunter made himself pay attention.

In fits and starts, with many pauses for breath, DeChance explained the history of the city, and what had happened there, and for the first time Hunter and Krystel understood the true nature of the aliens, and the significance of the copper tower. Hunter had a hundred questions he wanted to ask, but he didn't have the breath for even one. The tower suddenly loomed up before him at the end of the street, and he fixed his attention on that. The Squad pounded down the street, and skidded to a halt at the base of the tower. The two marines turned to face the pursuing aliens, and fired their disrupters. Several aliens fell screaming to the ground as the energy beams cut through them, and the rest of the pack fell on them. Hunter turned to find DeChance and the Investigator silently studying the copper tower.

"Well, don't just stand there. Get the bloody door open! The aliens will be here any minute!"

"We appear to have a problem, Captain," said the Investigator. "No door. No windows, either."

Hunter held up his field lantern and studied the tower closely for the first time. The great copper shaft stretched up into the night sky, featureless and immaculate save for the massive copper spikes that radiated from its peak. It looked to be thirty to forty feet in diameter, and maybe four hundred feet high. There was no trace of any opening in the gleaming metal, nor any sign there ever had been one. Hunter stepped forward and ran his hand across the metal. It felt preternaturally slick, almost frictionless.

"All right," he said quietly. "Stand back and watch out for flying metal." He fired his disrupter at the metal wall at point-blank range. The energy beam punched a tiny hole in the metal, and that was all.

"Great," said Corbie. "Now what?"

Hunter thought quickly. "Explosives. How many grenades have we got between us?"

He had one, Krystel had one, DeChance had two. The marines had used all theirs.

"That isn't going to be enough, Captain," said the Investigator. "The disrupter should have opened up the tower wall like a tin can. It didn't. A wall that strong isn't going to be bothered by concussion grenades. The force of the explosion would be too generalized."

"So what do you suggest?" snapped Corbie. "Kick the bloody thing? Or maybe we should knock politely and hope someone will let us in?"

"Keep the noise down, marine," said Hunter. "There is a way. We can use one of our proximity mines. That's powerful enough, and focused enough, to do the job. All we have to do is place one against the base of the tower wall, set the timer, and get the hell out of the way."

"That might just do it," said Lindholm approvingly. "Be a hell of a bang, anyway."

Hunter glanced quickly at the aliens. They'd stopped some distance away from the tower, and were watching silently. Presumably the great device didn't want them any closer, for its own security. Krystel produced a proximity mine from her backpack, put it in place, and set the timer. The Squad then moved quickly round to the far side of the tower. The explosion sounded strangely muffled, as though the tower had absorbed some of the blast, but when they went back to look they found a gaping hole in the tower wall, some five to six feet in diameter.

"We'd better tread carefully, once we get inside," said Krystel. "The blast may have damaged the device."

"It did," said DeChance. "But it's only superficial damage. I can feel the strength of the device. It burns in my mind like a beacon."

Hunter looked at her, and then at the two marines. They stirred uncomfortably.

"She has some kind of telepathic link with the device, Captain," said Lindholm slowly. "She thinks it's alive."

"And insane," said DeChance. "Quite definitely insane. I don't think it knows we're here yet, but it will the moment we enter the tower. I can't shield myself against that kind of power."

"This is all very interesting," said Hunter carefully, "but can you tell us anything more practical about the device?"

"Yes," said DeChance. "The explosion damaged one important part of the device. Try your comm unit, Captain. I think you'll find it's working again now."

Hunter gaped at her for a moment, and then tried his comm implant. It immediately patched him in with the pinnace computers, and for the first time that day Hunter felt complete again. Being cut off from the computers was like being cut off from his own memory. He gave the pinnace an update on what the Squad had discovered, and added a series of general orders for the computers to follow, if by some chance the Squad didn't make it back from the city. He checked the pinnace's power reserves and nodded slowly to himself. There was enough there to do what was needed. He dropped out of contact, and turned back to the Squad. They were talking animatedly as they discovered their comm units were working again too. Hunter coughed loudly to get their attention.

"All right, people. We're back in the game with a new deck. I've instructed the pinnace computers to warm up all the ship's systems. As soon as the ship's ready, I'll have the computers fly her here on remote control, and we'll get the hell out of this city."

"Sounds good to me," said Corbie. "The sooner we're out of here, the better."

"We can't leave," said DeChance.

"Try and stop me," said Corbie.

"The esper's right, Captain," said Krystel quickly. "For better or worse, this planet is our home now. We have to make our life here. And as long as this city and its creatures exist, we can never be safe. We can't communicate with them, and we can't live alongside them. They are insane, and as we have seen, quite deadly. It's us or them, Captain, and this may be the best chance we'll ever get to destroy them. They're dependent on this tower; if we destroy the great device, the aliens should die with it. If we leave the city now, we may never get another shot at the tower."

"You can't be sure of that," said Hunter. "And there's no guarantee that destroying the tower will destroy the aliens."

"Nothing's sure in this madhouse," said Krystel, "but it's our best bet."

"Yes," said Hunter finally. "I think it is." He patched into the pinnace computers again, fixed the flight plan, and set the engines in motion. "The ship's on its way, people. If we're going to destroy this tower, we'd better get a move on. You are sure the device is somewhere in this tower, DeChance?"

"The machine isn't in the tower, Captain," said the esper. "The machine *is* the tower. All of it."

She stepped through the jagged hole into the tower, holding her lantern up before her. Hunter and the others exchanged glances, and then followed her in. Outside in the night, the aliens tore savagely at each other, no longer interested in the Squad. The tower had them now.

Inside the copper tower there were huge shapes of metal and glass and crystal, fitted together in ways that made no sense to human eyes. Their dimensions seemed to vary according to which angle they were viewed from. There were parts that moved, and others that weren't always there, and there was a continuous low murmur of sound, as though the device were whispering secrets to itself. Hunter looked up into the tower, and saw the device stretching away above him; huge, cyclopean, and inhumanly intricate. Whoever, or whatever, had conceived the great device had a mind that worked on a different scale from humanity.

"This is it," said DeChance quietly. "This is the machine that freed the aliens from the tyranny of a fixed shape. This is where they made their own damnation."

"And it's still working, after who knows how many centuries," said Krystel.

"It's been asleep a long time," said DeChance. "It's awake now. And it knows we're here."

Hunter rubbed at his forehead. A vicious headache had started the moment he entered the tower. He felt hot and sweaty, and his fingers tingled uncomfortably.

"Are you all right, Captain?" asked Krystel quietly.

"I'm fine," said Hunter quickly. "Just the long day catching up with me."

"No," said DeChance. "It's the device. It's starting to work on us, now. It'll affect any living thing that stays within its influence too long. And the closer you are, the greater the effect is."

"Hey, wait a minute," said Corbie. "You mean we're going to turn into things like the aliens? Right. That's it. I'm off."

"Go outside on your own and the aliens will tear you to pieces," said DeChance. "But they won't come in here after us. The device wouldn't permit it. We're safe enough from the tower's influence for now. It takes time . . ." She held up her left hand and looked at it. The fingers had fused together into a single fleshy paw. "Of course, some of us are more susceptible than others."

Hunter looked at her closely, shocked, taking in the changes in her face since he'd last seen her. She'd definitely lost weight, and her bone structure was prominent almost to the point of emaciation. She stood awkwardly, and her stance was . . . different somehow. Changed. The marines hadn't noticed, because the changes had been slow and subtle, but they were clear enough now that Hunter was looking for them.

"How much longer can you stay here?" he asked softly. "Before the changes become . . . dangerous."

"I don't know. My esp makes me vulnerable, but you'll need that to help you find the device's weak spots. If it has any. The great device has survived for centuries without outside care or maintenance. It's bound to have self-defence mechanisms. I'm not even sure it can be destroyed with our feeble weapons. But we have to try." She looked around her. "There's a ramp nearby that leads up into the heart of the device. I think our best bet would be to plant our remaining explosives in the middle of the tower, or as close as we can get, and then make our escape on the pinnace before they blow." She looked at Hunter. "We'd better get moving, Captain. We don't have much time."

Hunter nodded soberly. "All right then, esper; lead the way. Investigator, you follow right behind her. Shoot anything that even looks threatening. The marines and I will bring up the rear. Shields on, guns and swords at the ready. Let's go, people."

DeChance moved confidently through the warren of enigmatic shapes, and stepped onto a simple ramp that led up into the heart of the machine. The rest of the Squad followed. Strange forms came and went around them as they trudged up the ramp, and Hunter began to feel like an insect that had become trapped in the workings of a machine it couldn't hope to understand. There was a kind of sense, of meaning, to the great device, but he could only recognise it without appreciating it. There were lights and sounds, and sudden rises and falls in temperature, and none of it made any sense.

The ramp wound between layers of shimmering crystal, and static sparked on the air. Hunter's headache grew worse, and his stomach felt increasingly uneasy. No doubt some of it was due to tension, but he couldn't help wondering how much of it might be caused by the device, and how long it would be before his body began changing, like DeChance's.

Metallic tentacles suddenly swung down from above, like writhing snakes. They seemed endless in the unsteady light, and they were tipped with reaching clawed hands. The Squad got their force shields up just in time, and the razor-sharp claws recoiled from the glowing energy fields. More tentacles came reaching out of nowhere, striking and retreating with inhuman speed. Hunter tried his sword against one of them, and the hilt jarred painfully in his hand as the steel blade sprang away without leaving a mark. The marines fired their guns, but the tentacles moved too quickly even for their experienced reflexes. The Investigator had used the edge of her shield to sever one tentacle, but the remaining tentacles avoided the shield's edges. It seemed they learned quickly. Blood flew on the air as the claws struck home, despite the force shields.

DeChance suddenly went down on one knee and hid behind her shield, eyes closed. Hunter moved quickly in beside her to protect her, but as far as he could see she hadn't been hurt. Her gaunt face was twisted with concentration, and in that moment she looked subtly inhuman to Hunter, as though an imperfect duplicate had taken the esper's place. DeChance's eyes snapped open, and Hunter's hackles rose on his neck. Her eyes were pools of bloodred, with long, split pupils.

"Three o'clock, Captain! Fire at three o'clock and you'll stop the defence mechanism!"

Hunter hesitated a moment, and then fired blindly where the esper indicated. There was an explosion somewhere up above, and the ramp shuddered under his feet. The tentacles disappeared back into the maze of machinery. The Squad slowly lowered their shields and looked around them. Hunter looked at DeChance, and did his best to meet her disquieting eyes.

"Very good, DeChance. Any more surprises we ought to know about?"

"Not yet, Captain, but we've got to move faster. The tower's influence is growing. I can feel it building. Soon you'll all start to change. Like me." Her voice had become harsh and strained, almost a growl. One arm was now clearly longer than the other. She smiled at Hunter, and her teeth had points. "It's not far now, Captain. I've located a weak spot where we can set our explosives."

She walked on up the ramp, and her body moved to an inhuman rhythm. Hunter's mouth was dry and sweat ran down his face. He wondered what the esper was becoming, and whether he was looking at his own future. Could he live, like that? Would he want to? He swallowed hard, and forced himself to concentrate on the business at hand. All that mattered now was setting the explosives and getting out of the city before they went off. He'd worry about anything else later. If there was a later.

They came to a place where thousands of wires seethed and writhed like a nest of worms. Electrical discharges skittered on the air. A crystal turned slowly in the midst of the wires, like a watchful eye.

"This is it," said DeChance. "I think it's some kind of relay. Blow this, and the whole tower will come down. If we're lucky."

"Lucky," said Corbie disgustedly. "I haven't felt lucky since we landed on this bloody planet."

The Squad set about emptying their backpacks, and between them they assembled a pile of proximity mines and grenades. The pile looked pitifully small, set against the vastness of the tower. Krystel arranged the explosives so as to do the most damage, and then checked the timers. She looked at Hunter, her face set and grim.

"Captain, we may have a problem here."

"Oh great," said Corbie. "Another problem. Just what we needed."

"Keep the noise down, Corbie," said Hunter. "What's the problem, Investigator?"

"The proximity mines, Captain. The timers have a maximum setting of thirty minutes. There's no way we can get out of here and reach a safe distance in thirty minutes."

Hunter frowned. "How far is a safe distance?"

"Unknown, Captain. But thirty minutes is barely enough time to get out of the tower."

Hunter looked at the esper. She shrugged; a quick, fluid gesture that disturbed Hunter greatly. "I can't say either, Captain. The great device affects every living thing on this planet, to some degree. There's no telling what will happen when we destroy it."

"The pinnace will be here soon," said Lindholm quietly. "This ship can get us out of the city in a matter of minutes."

"We'd still be cutting it too fine," said Hunter. "We have to leave a safety margin in case we run into any more defence mechanisms on our way back down the tower. No, there's only one answer to this problem. Someone will have to stay behind and set the explosives off by hand once the others have got away."

Corbie shook his head firmly. "Oh no. I don't volunteer for anything, and I'm not about to start now. Right, Sven?"

"Right," said Lindholm. "I don't believe in suicide missions. There has to be another way."

"There isn't," said the esper.

"I'm not asking for volunteers," said Hunter, his voice carefully calm and even. "I'm staying. It's my Squad, my duty."

"No, Captain," said DeChance. "I'm the one who has to stay."

"I am the Captain," said Hunter. "I won't betray my trust again."

"Very noble," said the esper in her rasping voice. "But not very practical. Look at me, Captain. *Look* at me."

She held up her right hand. It had twisted into a bony claw. The skin was covered with thick bristly hair. The arm that held it up was crooked where it should have been straight. And her face had become almost a caricature of what a human face should look like. She fixed Hunter with her alien eyes.

"The changes have gone too far, Captain. Do you think I want to live like this? You only see the obvious signs. There are changes inside me, too. And they're progressing. My esp makes me very susceptible to the tower's influence. Get out of here, Captain. Take the Squad and get the hell out of here. I'll give you an hour, before I set the timers. That should be enough."

Hunter nodded, not trusting himself to speak for a moment. "I'll tell the colonists all about you, Megan. I promise." He turned to Krystel. "Investigator, lead the way back down the ramp."

The Squad made quick, quiet good-byes to the esper, and left. She lowered herself carefully onto the ramp, and sat there alone in the light from her field lantern. For a while she listened to the Squad's departing footsteps, but they soon disappeared under the constant murmurings of the great device. She felt very tired. She watched the electrical discharges fluttering on the air, and listened to the machinery as it muttered around her like so many unspoken thoughts.

The Investigator led the Squad back down through the tower. There were no more sudden attacks, no more defence mechanisms. They came to the hole in the base of the tower wall, and Hunter gestured for the Squad to stay put while he took a look outside. He peered warily out into the night, and his stomach fell away. For as far as he could see, the copper tower was surrounded by an endless sea of monsters. Creatures varying in size from ten feet high to a dozen yards long waited silently in ranks beyond number. They did not move or speak or fight each other. The great device had called to them and they had come, impelled and controlled by its silent voice. Hunter ducked back inside the tower.

"We have a problem, people."

"What, another one?" said Corbie. "What is it this time?"

"Take a look outside, one at a time," said Hunter. He waited patiently while they did. Afterwards, even the Investigator looked more than usually grim. "The aliens are quiet for the moment," said Hunter finally. "But once we step outside the tower the odds are they'll go crazy."

"But why are they waiting?" said Lindholm. "They're not even fighting each other."

"The tower's influence must be growing," said Krystel. "Captain, we'll have to tell the esper we need more time.

We're trapped in here until we can think of a way out of this mess."

"There is a way out," said Hunter. "But it's going to call for some split-second timing. The pinnace will be here shortly. There's just enough room out there for it to land. I'll open the airlock by remote control, and we make a dash for it."

"The aliens will be on us pretty quick," said Corbie. "What happens if one of us trips and falls?"

"Don't," said Hunter.

"I hate this planet," said Corbie. "I really hate it."

"We've still got a problem," said Lindholm. "Theoretically, there's room out there for the pinnace to land, but in reality, it's too tricky a landing for remote control. Much more likely we'd crash the ship trying. We need more space."

"Then we'll make some," said Krystel. She smiled, and hefted her sword.

"No," said Hunter, thinking quickly. "There are too many aliens this time. If we stand and fight they'll sweep right over us. There's a better way. About half a mile from here there's a wide-open square. Plenty of room for the pinnace to land. I'll set her down there by remote control, and then we'll make a dash for her. If we're quick enough and mean enough, we should just make it."

"Let me see if I've got this straight," said Corbie. "We're going to have to fight our way through half a mile of aliens, just to reach the pinnace?"

"That's right," said Krystel. "Bearing in mind all the time that the esper's clock is running. If we take too long getting there, it won't matter anyway."

"I hate this planet," said Corbie.

"It's not quite as desperate as it sounds," said Hunter. "Outside and to the right, there's a narrow alleyway between two buildings. If we hit the aliens hard enough we should be able to punch right through them and straight into the alley. They'll only be able to come after us in ones and twos, and we can make straight for the open square, and the pinnace. All right, that's enough chatter. Let's get moving, while our nerve holds out."

• • •

In the heart of the great device, silent and alone, sat the quiet, desperate thing that had once been Megan DeChance. The device was playing with her now. One of her arms had become rotten and corrupt. In the other, her bones had become soft and limp. She still had feelings in some of her fingers. She hoped there was enough left for her to set the timers. She looked again at the timepiece embedded in what was left of her right wrist. It was getting hard to concentrate. She hoped she could hold out long enough to give the Squad the hour she'd promised them, but didn't know if she could.

She was changing more and more rapidly now that she was so close to the device. Her humanity was fading away in fits and starts. She couldn't even tell which changes came from the device, and which came from her own subconscious mind. Her skin had a dozen textures, and her bones no longer held their shapes. She could feel strange organs growing inside her. She didn't know yet what their purpose was. It was getting harder to think. Her thoughts were becoming vague and unclear and tinged with alien colors. She tried to say her name aloud, but her voice only made sounds, not all of them human. It was time. If she left it any longer, she might not remember what to do. She hoped, fleetingly, that the Squad had got out of range, and then she reached carefully out to set the timer on the first mine. She couldn't do it. The fingers on her right hand had become too large and clumsy to work the settings. She couldn't even prime it. She looked at her left hand. It was a shapeless fleshy paw. The explosives were useless. She couldn't set them off. The thing that had once been Megan DeChance raised its misshapen head and howled its anguish. The sound wasn't at all human.

Hunter burst out of the copper tower and ran for the narrow alleyway. He raised his disrupter, and a beam of searing energy smashed through the hulking creature before him. It swept on to pierce three other shapes before a fourth finally absorbed the beam. The aliens roared and howled as the

smell of blood hit the air, and in seconds they had turned
on each other, their single-minded emotions overpowering
the tower's hold on them. Hunter and Krystel charged
into the alleyway, opening up a space with their swords
and shields. Corbie and Lindholm followed close behind,
using their guns on creatures distracted from attacking
their injured fellows. The extra blood sent the aliens into
a feeding frenzy. Teeth and claws tore at uncertain flesh
as the Hell Squad cut their way through the chaos to reach
the narrow alleyway, their progress slowed but not stopped
by creatures who no longer knew how to die.

Something tall and angular with flailing whips of bone
and gristle lashed out at Hunter, bringing him to an abrupt
halt. He met the whips with his shield, and they rebounded
harmlessly from the glowing energy field. The alien tried
to grab the shield with its whips, and the razor-sharp edges
cut through them instantly. The alien paused uncertainly,
and Hunter cut through its narrow neck with one sweep
of his sword. The headless body attacked the creature
next to it, its whips flailing blindly. The elongated head
rolled away down the street, its mouth still snapping, until
another creature pounced on it. Krystel swung her sword
double-handed at Hunter's side, driving the aliens back
with the sheer speed and energy and viciousness of her
attack. Blood soaked her from head to foot, little of it her
own, and her grinning teeth flashed white in the bloody
mask of her face. This was where she belonged, where
she felt most alive; in the heart of conflict. She took some
wounds despite her skills, but she barely felt them. She was
beyond pain now. There was only her sword and her shield,
and an endless supply of victims.

Corbie and Lindholm fought back to back, cutting down
anything that came within reach. The ex-gladiator fought
silently and efficiently, inflicting the maximum damage
with the least effort. That was the way of the Arena; to
save one's strength for when it was needed. Corbie danced
and stamped and thrust, howling threats and curses. Mostly
he cursed having run out of grenades. A silver creature
with too many legs dropped onto him from a nearby wall.

Corbie knocked it to one side with his shield, and skewered it while it lay thrashing on its back on the ground.

Hunter finally plunged into the narrow alleyway, with the rest of the Squad close behind. The press of aliens fell away as the high-walled buildings on either side protected them from the mass of the ravenous horde. Something flat and leathery swept down from above. Corbie deflected it with a quick shot from his disrupter, but only burned a hole through one membranous wing. Krystel shot it in the head, and it fell limply to the ground. Corbie and Lindholm trampled it underfoot, and threw the body out of the alley to the blood-mad aliens. They blocked off the alley mouth as they tore at the flapping creature. Hunter looked down the far end of the alley, and his heart sank. A mass of alien shapes blocked it off, and the first few were already heading down the alley towards the Squad. Hunter slowed to a halt. The Squad crowded in behind him. Corbie looked to see what the problem was, and swore briefly.

"We're trapped, aren't we?" said Lindholm.

"Looks that way," said Hunter. "We'll just have to fight our way out, that's all. It's only half a mile to the open square, and by the time we get there the pinnace should be waiting for us."

The Hell Squad formed a defensive wall of force shields, and moved steadily down the alley to meet the waiting aliens.

What was left of Megan DeChance crawled slowly along the ramp. It could only move slowly now, and it left a trail behind it. It wanted to go after the Squad, to warn them that it couldn't set off the explosives, but even that simple task was beyond it now. The device's influence was growing, and the creature's body was falling apart. Its flesh ran like melting wax down a candle, and its fingers dripped skin. The only things it had left that still worked properly were its implants. The thought struck a spark in the creature somewhere, and it fought to concentrate on it. The comm implant, the computers, the pinnace . . . Something that was meant to be a smile twisted its face. It still had one last hope, one last weapon to throw at the copper tower.

It activated the comm implant, and patched into the pinnace computers. It took only a few moments to take over the remote control, and give the pinnace a new heading and destination. The creature laughed silently, and crawled slowly over to the nearest wall. It took some time to draw the disrupter from its holster and aim it at the wall. It took even longer before it found a way to press the stud with what was left of its fingers, but eventually the energy beam tore a hole through the tower wall, and the creature could look out at the darkness. Out in the night, a bright star grew slowly larger as the pinnace headed for the copper tower.

The aliens pressed close around the embattled Squad, driving forward from both ends of the alley at once. Hunter and Krystel fought side by side, striking down things that had no place in the waking world. The two marines fought together with bitter competence. They were both experienced enough fighters to know that this was one battle they couldn't win. The aliens could be hurt and damaged and even thrown back temporarily, but their wounds healed in seconds, and they could not die. They still fought and tore at each other, but now it was in eagerness to get at the Squad.

Hunter saw the disrupter blast that tore a hole through the side of the copper tower, and thought for a moment the explosives had gone off early. It took only a quick glance to see that the damage was merely superficial. He wondered what the hell the esper thought she was doing, but the aliens pushed forward again, and for a while he lost himself in the press of battle. He was slowing down as his muscles cramped, fatigue hanging like lead weights on his arms, and even his force shield couldn't protect him from every attack. And then a low, continuous roar made itself heard above the sound of battle, and Hunter risked a hopeful glance up at the night sky. The pinnace came sweeping over the city from the east, its engines thundering on the night, its hull shining bright with navigation lights.

Hunter's heart surged with hope, and he fought with a new ferocity.

What remained of Megan DeChance watched the pinnace soar across the city, and tried to laugh. It was the creature's last act of defiance against the thing that was destroying it, and it was a good one. It cried, and its tears dug furrows in its face, like acid. The pinnace thundered across the city, heading straight for the copper tower. The creature gave one last command through its comm implant, and laughed silently as its form finally collapsed. The pinnace's engines roared as they moved to full power, and the ship leaped forward to slam into the copper tower at full speed. The great device screamed through the throats of the undying aliens as the pinnace's engines exploded, shattering the copper tower and tearing apart the insane mechanism that had made the city a living hell. The explosion seemed to echo endlessly on the night, and when it finally died away, the city was still and silent, save for the flickering flames around the base of the broken copper tower.

CHAPTER EIGHT

Aftermath

HUNTER awoke in a sea of grey jelly. It clung stickily to him as he sat up, and fell reluctantly away from his uniform. The stuff even coated his hands, and he shook it off with a *moue* of distaste. His head ached, his joints were stiff, and all in all he hadn't felt this tired since Basic Training. He looked slowly around him in the early morning light, and wondered fleetingly how long he'd been unconscious. And then the previous night came flooding back, and he scrambled to his feet. He looked wildly around him, and only then realised there was no sign anywhere of the army of monstrosities he'd been fighting.

He was standing in the middle of what was left of the narrow alleyway, and all around him lay great pools and streamers of the thick grey jelly. It looked to be two or three inches deep in places, and it smelled awful. Not far away, Corbie and Lindholm were sitting with their backs to the wall, talking softly. They looked bruised and bloodied, but pretty much intact. They saw Hunter looking at them, and managed something like a salute. Hunter nodded briefly, and looked at what was left of the alley walls. The copper tower had contained most of its own explosion, and the high walls on either side of the alleyway had soaked up the rest of the blast.

How about that? thought Hunter. *We finally had some good luck.*

The Investigator was standing at the entrance to the alleyway, staring out at the city. Hunter made his way over to her, treading carefully so as not to slip in the

183

jelly. Krystel heard him coming, and looked back over her shoulder.

"Good morning, Captain. Welcome back to the living. I think you'd better come and take a look at this. It's really very interesting."

Hunter felt a brief stab of foreboding. The Investigator usually found things interesting only if they involved violence or imminent sudden death. He moved forward to join her, frowning slightly as he took in Krystel's blood-soaked uniform. It wasn't until he'd come to a halt beside her that he realised most of the blood and gore wasn't hers. *I should have known,* he thought wryly. *She's an Investigator.* And then he frowned again, and looked more closely as he took in the traces of grey jelly on her uniform. Krystel smiled.

"Not very pleasant stuff, is it? You'll find most of it brushes off."

"How did it get on our uniforms?" said Hunter, brushing determinedly at his sleeves.

"I think we spent most of the night sleeping in it, Captain. The destruction of the device in the copper tower apparently knocked us out for some time. As to where the jelly came from . . . take a look at the city."

Hunter looked, and his tiredness suddenly fell away as his adrenaline kicked in. There was no sign of any of the aliens, living or dead, but the grey jelly was everywhere. The vile-smelling stuff carpeted the streets, and spattered the sides of buildings. It hung in syrupy streamers from windows and bridges, and flapped loosely on the breeze. Hunter heard the two marines come up behind him, but he didn't look round.

"Now that really is disgusting," said Corbie. "What the hell is this stuff?"

"Take a good look," said Krystel. "I think this slime is all that's left of the aliens."

Hunter looked at her blankly for a moment, and then nodded slowly as he made the connection. "Of course; when the forest was attacked, it lost its shape and melted into jelly. So did those plant creatures we met before the forest. The esper said all along that only the great device was keeping the aliens alive, and that's gone now." He looked across at the fire-blackened ruins of the copper tower. "The device had to weaken their physical bonds to make shape-changing possible, but it weakened their bodies so much that in the end only the device was holding them together. When the pinnace destroyed the tower, the aliens just fell apart, collapsing back into the simple primordial jelly from which all life begins. The aliens are gone, all of them. And they won't be coming back."

The Squad stood in silence for a while, staring out over the silent city.

"I wonder what went wrong with the esper," said Lindholm finally. "Why didn't she set off the explosives?"

Hunter shrugged. "I don't suppose we'll ever know. Perhaps the device rendered the explosives useless in some way. Without them, all she had left was her comm link with the pinnace, and her own determination. She was a very brave woman, at the end."

"Fine," said Corbie. "We'll build her a statue. Look, far be it from me to sound ungrateful, but what about us? How are we supposed to survive without the equipment in the pinnace? We can't even call for help with our main comm system destroyed!"

"Relax, Corbie," said Hunter calmly. "When I first re-established contact with the pinnace, I took the opportunity to order the computers to pass on a summary of everything we'd found. And since the Empire's always interested in new alien civilisations, I think we can expect a fully equipped starship any time in the next few weeks. We should be able to survive that long on our own. In fact, with the aliens and their device gone, this could turn out to be quite a pleasant little world."

"Pleasant, but boring," said Krystel, lighting up her carefully hoarded last cigar.

"I can live with boring," said Corbie. "There's a lot to be said for boring as a way of life."

"You should know," said Lindholm.

"And there's always the city," said Hunter. "There's enough mysteries and new technologies here to keep us busy for years. We won't have any problems attracting colonists for Wolf IV; scientists and their families will be fighting tooth and nail for the chance to examine this city. After all, there's one very important question still to be answered."

He waited, smiling, and eventually Corbie sighed heavily.

"All right, Captain, I'll bite. What very important question?"

"According to the pinnace computers," said Hunter, "this is the only city on the planet. Which implies the aliens didn't originate here. They came to Wolf IV the same way we did; as colonists. But if that's true, where is the aliens' home planet, and why didn't they come back to check up on their colony? I'm sure the Empire will want to know. After all, a species sufficiently advanced to build something like the great device could end up as the Empire's first real rival."

Captain Hunter smiled. "I don't think we'll find life here too boring, people. There are enough mysteries here to keep us busy for the rest of our lives."